W9-BWG-551

THE
CONTENDER

THE CONTENDER

by
Robert Lipsyte

HarperCollins*Publishers*

THE CONTENDER

Copyright © 1967 by Robert M. Lipsyte

All rights reserved. No part of this book may be used or reproduced in any manner whatsoever without written permission except in the case of brief quotations embodied in critical articles and reviews. Printed in the United States of America. For information address HarperCollins Children's Books, a division of HarperCollins Publishers, 10 East 53rd Street, New York, NY 10022.

Library of Congress Catalog Card Number: 67-19623
ISBN 0-06-023919-0
ISBN 0-06-023920-4 (lib. bdg.)

For my mother and father

THE
CONTENDER

CHAPTER 1

He waited on the stoop until twilight, pretending to watch the sun melt into the dirty gray Harlem sky. Up and down the street transistor radios clicked on and hummed into the sour air. Men dragged out card tables, laughing. Cars cruised through the garbage and broken glass, older guys showing off their Friday night girls. Another five minutes, he thought. I'll give James another five minutes.

"You still here, Alfred?" Aunt Pearl came out on the stoop, her round face damp from the kitchen.

He tried to sound casual. "You know James. He better hurry or we'll miss the first picture."

"He's never been this late, Alfred. Why don't you go upstairs and call his house? Maybe he's sick."

"James ain't sick." Alfred stood up.

"How you know that?" Her eyes narrowed. "You know where he's at?"

"Maybe."

"He's hangin' out with those worthless punks, ain't he, Alfred? Maybe you just better . . . Alfred!"

But he was already off the stoop and moving fast, his sneakers slapping on the sidewalk. Packs of little kids, raggedy and skinny, raced past him along the gutter's edge, kicking empty beer cans ahead of them. Used to do that too, when we were little, he thought. One thing I could always do better than James. I was always faster. Big deal. He slowed down.

He stopped at the mouth of the alley, and took a deep breath. What am I, James' shadow or something? I don't need him. But he marched to the basement steps, and plunged down into the clubroom.

Hollis and Sonny were sprawled on the long, sagging couch, snapping their fingers to a scratchy record. Major was flexing his arm muscles at the cracked mirror over the mop sink. Only James, trying to read a magazine in the dim light of the naked bulb, looked up.

"Hey, man, what's happening?"

"Nothing much," said Alfred. "Ready to go to the movies?"

"Not unless it's free night," said James.

"I got some money," said Alfred.

Major turned slowly and let his muscles relax. "How much you got, Alfred?"

Sonny and Hollis stopped snapping.

"I said, 'How much you got, Alfred?' "

"Nothing," mumbled Alfred, staring down at the tips of his sneakers.

"You the only one workin', and you got paid today," said Major. "What you got?"

"Gave it to my aunt," said Alfred.

"'Gave it to my aunt,'" mimicked Major. "You such a good sweet boy. Old Uncle Alfred."

Sonny giggled, and Hollis grinned, buck-toothed. James looked away.

"Don't you know this club has got dues?" Major folded his arms across his bulging T-shirt.

Hollis leaned back in the couch. "Go collect the dues, Sonny. Turn Alfred upside down and make the dues fall out his pockets."

"'Turn Alfred upside down,'" echoed Sonny, blankly. He stood up, taller than any of them and almost as heavily muscled as Major. "Upside down."

"Hold on," said James. "Alfred's my guest. I invited him to come down."

Alfred took a step backward, nearly knocking over an old wooden chair. "Let's go, James."

Major swaggered across the room, the metal tips on his pointed shoes clicking on the concrete floor. "How much them Jews give you for slavin', Uncle Alfred?"

"Jews squeeze the eagle till it screams," said Hollis. "The eagle screams, 'Faster, Alfred, sweep that floor, you skinny nigger.'"

"They been all right to me," said Alfred.

"How come you ain't workin' right now?" said Major, circling until he stood between Alfred and the door.

"Grocery's closed."

"At eight o'clock?"

"They close early on Friday to go to synagogue."

3

"They go pray for more dollars," said Hollis. Even James smiled.

"No," said Alfred. "The Epsteins are very religious. They don't even touch money after sundown on Fridays."

"That's a lie," said Major.

"No. They even leave money in the cash register so they won't have to . . ." He bit his lip. Water dripped into the mop sink, small explosions in the suddenly silent room.

"Let's get it," whispered Hollis.

"Show us," said Major.

"No, I—"

"You just a slave," sneered Major. "You was born a slave. You gonna die a slave."

" 'Slave,' " echoed Sonny.

"I see you now, boy, old and stooped," said Major, shuffling to the center of the room. "Old and stooped. You be scratching your head and saying, 'Yassuh, Mistuh Lou, lemme brush them hairs offen your coat; yassuh, Mistuh Jake, I be pleased iffen you 'low me to wash your car.' "

Sonny and Hollis began to laugh as Major shuffled around the dim, warm room, his muscular arms dangling like a monkey's, his eyes rolling, his black head bobbing in ugly imitation of an old-time Negro servant. "I can see you now, Alfred, good old Uncle Alfred. 'Yassuh, Mistuh Ben, I be so grat-i-fied iffen you'd kick me now and again, show how much you white folks love us.' "

4

The laughter rose, high-pitched and nervous. Alfred peeked at their faces, black and sweating in the semicircle around him. Hollis and Sonny, grinning and nodding. James' chubby face was set and unsmiling as Major continued his imitation, scratching his nose, pouting his lips, and shambling loosely like a puppet at the end of jerking strings.

Alfred's hands were wet.

"You come on with us," said James. "You know just where to—"

"We don't need him if he's scared," said Hollis.

"He isn't scared, not him," said James. "Look, Alfred, you don't owe them anything."

"They gave me a job," said Alfred, surprised at how far away his own voice sounded.

"Big job," said Hollis.

"Yassuh," yelled Major, shuffling back into the center. "'Mistuh Lou, I been sweepin' out your store forty year now, how 'bout lettin' me de-li-ver groceries on the bi-cy-cle oncet in a while?' "

Alfred swallowed hard. "They was the only ones gave me a job when I quit school," he yelled.

They fell quiet again.

"You come on, Alfred," said James, softly. "Whitey been stealing from us for three hundred years. We just going to take some back."

"No."

"You could stay outside, be lookout," said James.

Major shouldered in between them. "You coming?"

Alfred shook his head.

5

"Let's go," said Major, moving toward the door. He turned at the first step, Sonny and Hollis at his heels. "James?"

"Let's go to the movies, James," said Alfred.

"That's all you ever want to do," said James.

They stared at each other.

"You coming, James, or you gonna be a slave too?"

James turned away. He followed the others up the steps to the street. The door banged shut behind them. Fool, thought Alfred. Had to open your mouth. He kicked the chair across the room.

"Good kick, man. Where's everybody going in such a hurry?" Henry limped down into the clubroom, dragging his crippled left leg, the perpetual grin spread across his skinny face.

Alfred shrugged.

"Play some cards?"

"I gotta go, Henry."

"Hey, Alfred, you know what I'm doing now? Mr. Donatelli, the fight manager, he's letting me . . . Where you going?"

"Out."

The stench of wine and garbage still hung in the moist June air. He jammed his hands into the pockets of his tight blue slacks, watching the cars cruise past. Another year, he thought, be eighteen, able to drive. Sure. On grocery-boy pay. Slave. The bells of the ice cream truck jangled across the street, and a sudden roar burst from a dozen transistor radios. Somebody must have hit a home run. The Epsteins would be in their synagogue now, wearing skull caps and praying. He started to walk toward his house, then stopped. Aunt Pearl would be sitting on the stoop, waving the fan the undertaker gave away at summer funerals. She would ask him why he wasn't with James. She would know if he was lying. He went back down to the clubroom.

Henry was punching at his reflection in the cracked mirror. He dropped his hands when he saw Alfred, and the big grin turned sheepish.

"Shadowboxing," he said.

"Yeah."

"Mr. Donatelli's letting me work around the gym, take care of the gloves and wash the mouthpieces."

"Big job."

"You ought to come up, Alfred. Willie Streeter's training now. He's going to fight in Madison Square Garden next week."

"Yeah."

"Lotta guys come up and train," said Henry.

"Yeah."

"Hey, man, where you—"

Out on the street again, he idly watched a green-and-white police cruiser slide by, a thick, hairy white arm hanging out of the open window. Alfred stiffened. The burglar alarm, the new silent burglar alarm installed at Epsteins' the other night. How could I forget about that? They'd never hear it go off. It would ring in the detectives' office, and they'd call the police right away.

He began to run. Got to get to James, got to tell James. But the radio inside the police car began to crackle and sputter, as if it had read his mind. The car suddenly picked up speed.

Silently, a second police car joined the first. Then both wheeled around the corner, roaring into noise and light, motors growling, headlights glaring, sirens howling. Alfred slowed down as hundreds of people came off stoops and street corners, and poured out of bars toward four cruisers parked behind Epsteins'. The doors of the police cars were open, and the red roof lights were blinking.

He heard shouts, and a voice yelled, "Stop, stop." A shot rang out. The warning shot.

He started running again, toward the shot, but the crowd thickened in front of him. "They caught one," someone yelled from an upstairs window. The crowd surged forward, sweeping Alfred along. He tried to push through, but the crowd was too tightly packed.

"The Man," mumbled a voice off to his left. "Always lookin' to put his foot on a black throat."

"You sayin' the truth, brother."

"Only reason po-lice up here to watch out for them white stores."

"So right."

Police car doors slammed shut, and the cruisers drove away, their sirens on. The crowd began to drift back to their stoops, to the drinks they had left on bars. Alfred passed an old man who lived in his building, and grabbed his arm.

"You see who they caught?"

The old man shook his head. "They hustled him away too fast."

"Just one?"

"A couple got away."

Alfred pushed his way out of the crowd, and onto a side street. He had to think. The three who got away would split up and hide. If James made it, there would be only one place for him to go. Alfred circled toward the park, his hands in his pockets, his head low. He kept his feet moving slowly. Police cars cruised by, and he felt eyes staring out at him. Keep walking slow.

It was quiet in the park. Couples were drinking and whispering on the grass, and the transistors were turned down. He saw the rock, big as a truck, outlined against a purple-black sky, and his feet moved faster, over the small rocks, over the low thicket of bushes. He dropped to his knees and wriggled through the tangle of stunted, twisted trees that hid the opening beneath the huge rock. On his elbows, he crawled into the cave.

He had forgotten how small it was. He could barely sit up. The thin layer of loose dirt on the flat rock floor was cool against his palms, and his head touched the jagged rock ceiling. He drew his knees up to his chest, and held them. He slowed his breathing, and strained his ears for James.

He tried to remember the first time he had been in the cave. Ten years ago. James was there, too. He was hardly ever in the cave without James—Alfred squeezed against the back, James up front, poking out his head to

9

see if the coast was clear. They were just little kids then, running away from older boys, like Major, who tried to hold them up for nickels on the street. They'd break and run when they saw Major coming, circle around till they were out of sight, then sprint into the park. They'd scramble through the underbrush into the cave, shaking and out of breath, clapping their hands over each other's mouths to muffle their laughter. After a while, James might start his imitations. He would be Mrs. McCormick, their public school principal, pressing his lips together until they almost disappeared, fluttering his eyelids. "Chil-dren. With-out ed-u-ca-tion man is a sav-age beast." They'd collapse into hiccuping laughter.

And then James might screw up his face and make his eyes bulge, like Rick, the white college boy who ran the summer program. "Gotta hang in there, guys. Can't lose if you hang in there." They liked Rick, who showed them how professional basketball players took foul shots, and how to throw curve balls. They were getting good too, until Major and Sonny and Hollis began hanging around the playground, making remarks and kicking balls out of their hands. One summer Rick just didn't come back.

A twig snapped outside.

"James?" he whispered.

There was a soft, scampering sound, then quiet again. Squirrel.

James had found the cave the summer they were rock

hunting. James had a library book on rocks, and they spent days just wandering around the park, filling their pockets with little rocks that matched the pictures in the book. For a while they kept their rocks in the cave, and then James took them home. He was going to arrange them in a cardboard box and bring them to school in September. James' father came home drunk one night and dropped all the rocks down the air shaft.

Far away, a police siren whined. Alfred shivered. C'mon, James, make it, man, get away. He moved his head, and dirt fell off the ceiling of the cave into his eyes and mouth.

He remembered the night his own father left home forever. He was ten. James sat with him then, in the cave. They talked, and it made him feel a little better. And James was there three years later when Alfred's mother died of pneumonia in the city hospital, sitting with him all night, whispering, "Gonna be all right, Alfred. I'm gonna stick by you. We're partners, right?" Then they crawled out of the cave, and James walked him back to his new home with Aunt Pearl and her three little daughters.

C'mon, James, where are you? Alfred's legs began to cramp and stiffen. Tears streamed down his cheeks.

James tried to talk him into staying in school. "Can't get a good job without that piece of paper, Alfred." James was going to be an engineer, and build things. Alfred could help him. They'd make a fortune and drive back to the neighborhood in a white Cadillac, and go right to the cave, crawl on the ground in their silk suits, and pull out any little kids they found in there and buy them something really fine. Never happen now. I quit school, and after all that talk, James quits four months later.

He pinched his calves to stop his legs from falling asleep. Five minutes, give him another five minutes.

James didn't even look for a job, started hanging around with Major and Hollis, believing them when they said the white man would never let him build anything but garbage heaps. He started going to the clubroom in the basement of the building where Henry's father was superintendent. Maybe the partnership started busting up then. If only James had come to the movies tonight, like every other Friday night. And that burglar alarm—how could I forget about that burglar alarm?

He moved his head again, and tasted more dirt. Maybe the police caught James. Or maybe he got away, and had a better place to hide now. With Major.

Slowly, he crawled out.

It was pitch-dark. The big rock was hard to see against the black sky. The transistors were silent. He crept carefully, until no one who might be watching could tell where he had come from. Then he stood up and walked toward home. The side streets were quieter now. His legs began to lose their stiffness. He turned down his street.

"Why it's good old Uncle Alfred."

He froze. Major's arms were folded across his chest,

and Hollis' lips were pulled back in a buck-toothed grin.

"Where's James?"

" 'Where's James?' " mimicked Major.

"They caught him, you . . . " snarled Hollis, pushing Sonny toward Alfred, and then the four of them were in a tight pile of swinging arms and legs, kicking, cuffing, punching, and Alfred smashed into the pavement, under Sonny, and the elbows and fists began crashing into his sides, his head, his stomach.

"You knew 'bout that alarm," grunted Major, hammering down on him.

"I forgot, I would of . . . " Alfred tasted his own blood, warm and salty, and he felt the pavement scrape the skin off his shoulder blades. He struggled, trying to kick upwards, but the three of them were too much, bearing down, slugging, stomping . . .

"Split," hissed Major, and they were standing. "We'll get you . . . " and they were gone.

Far down the block, two patrolmen, one black, one white, walked lightly, looking over each other's shoulders, glancing up at the rooftops. Alfred dragged himself into an alley, and crawled painfully behind a garbage can. He swallowed back his nausea as a rat scurried over his arm, squealing. The two policemen whirled at the sound, hands on their guns. They looked at each other, shrugged, and walked on. Alfred fainted.

CHAPTER 2

He woke up in his aunt's bed, blinking against the white glare of the morning sun. He felt her calloused hand move gently over his swollen jaw long before he saw her red-rimmed eyes peering down at him.

"How do you feel, Alfred, honey?" Her voice, usually so warm and light, sounded husky and tired.

"I'm okay, Aunt Pearl."

"Thank the Lord." She lowered herself to the edge of the narrow bed. "We was so scared for you, Alfred. Prayed all night, prayed to God and to your sweet momma, rest her soul, got right down on—"

"It's okay, Aunt Pearl, I'm okay." He moved his legs under the sheet, then his arms. Numb, aching pain everywhere, but everything moving, nothing broken.

"What happened, Alfred? When Henry and Mister Johnson carried you—"

"Henry?"

"He found you. You was wandering around with your

14

eyes shut, and he went and got his daddy to help carry you home. What happened, Alfred?"

"The, uh, old stone fence off Lenox, Aunt Pearl. I was walking on it, and . . . a . . . a big dog jumped up. Knocked me off."

"Uh, huh," she said, but he could see by her eyes she knew he was lying. She turned, and he saw his three little cousins jammed in the doorway, staring at him. "You heard what happened, now you go out and play. Go ahead, give Alfred a chance to rest. Charlene, you be sure you're all back for supper. Mrs. Elversen's havin' a party, and I'll be bringin' home all kinds of good things."

The twins began to edge back, but Charlene kept staring. It seemed to Alfred that her eyes were red-rimmed, too. "Go on, now."

Aunt Pearl waited until they had clattered out of the apartment and down the tenement stairs before she turned back to Alfred. She was frowning. "James was arrested last night, Alfred. For trying to break into Epsteins'."

"I know."

"You knew about it, him going?"

"Yes."

"But you wasn't with him, that right?"

"That's right."

"He wanted you to go, that right?"

When he didn't answer, she leaned closer. "Who beat you, Alfred?"

"I fell off the fence."

She shook her head, her hands again on his aching face. "Oh, Alfred, it's like you're my own son. I know you try so hard, you so good. I know it ain't easy, living here. Someday, someday we're gonna move away, Alfred, and we . . ." She began to cry, softly.

After a while she rose and smoothed the front of her cotton dress. "I got to work now, Alfred. Be back about eight tonight. You rest. There's some food by the bed, you eat something right now."

She paused at the door, and forced a smile. Weakly, he waved back, and slipped again into sleep.

It was noon when he awoke again. His head felt clear. The pain in his arms and legs seemed to have eased. Biting carefully on aching teeth, he ate the bread and cheese and baloney she had left by the bed, and drank some of the milk, now warm. Street sounds floated up through the open window, children yelling, the thud of a rubber ball against the pavement, four voices singing, "Hey, bay-bee, you're num-ber one, you're . . . ," cars honking Saturday strollers out of their way. Far off, he heard a police siren knife through the street noise. He felt it in his belly.

James was in jail. He burrowed deeper into the bed. It was his fault, letting it slip about the money in the cash register. His fault again for not remembering about the new burglar alarm. Nice bed, soft and safe, away from all of them, he thought. Major and Hollis out on the street, looking to get me. The Epsteins, they'll be asking questions on Monday morning. They know James is my best friend. *Was* my best friend. No partner, nothing. Stay in bed, man, curl up like a baby, close your eyes, make the world go away. The big white world full of cans to stack and floors to sweep and pails of garbage to drag out back. Big job. Maybe James was right to try to get some of that money, only wrong to get caught. Just stay in bed, man, until you're eighteen, then join the Army. No, stay in bed forever.

He made himself get up then, pushing his long, wiry legs over the edge of the bed, standing on the little throw rug until the quivering stopped. He went into the bathroom, and patted cold water on his face before he looked at himself in the mirror. There were specks of dried blood on his hair. His left eye was swollen and bloodshot. His bony face was puffy, especially around the jaw and lips. There was a long scratch down the side of his nose, and another high on his right cheek. Not so bad. Looked worse that time I really fell off the stone fence. He grinned. Major and Hollis, for all their talk, they can't even rob a store or beat up a guy right. Just punks. Then he remembered that James was in jail, and the grin disappeared.

He walked into the front room, and sat down on the worn couch that opened into a double bed for Charlene and the twins. He turned on the television set.

A slim, pretty, white woman was standing in a shiny kitchen as big as Aunt Pearl's apartment, telling her tall, handsome husband how worried she was about Billy.

He was spending all his free time in the garage and he wouldn't let anybody in except Gus, the dog. The husband puffed on his pipe and said he'd look into it, dear, and went outside, walking across a big lawn and under trees. He knocked on the garage door. Billy yelled, Who's there? Dad yelled back, The F.B.I., and there was tinny sounding laughter. Billy yelled, Just a minute, Dad, and there he was, about fourteen, scrambling around trying to hide the robot he was building. . . .

"Yeah, sure," said Alfred, snapping off the television.

He went back into his aunt's bedroom. The four voices on the street were getting louder ". . . num-ber one, on my top ten, you're . . . ," but as soon as Alfred's head touched the pillow he was falling again into sleep.

The third time he awoke it was dusk. An occasional peal of drunken laughter drowned out the hoarse yells of tired children and the stoop chatter and the muted noise of a dozen transistors on different stations. He got up and went into the kitchen, enjoying the coolness of the cracked linoleum under his bare feet. The foldaway bed he usually slept in was tucked behind the refrigerator. He wondered if Aunt Pearl had slept in it, or stayed up all night. The sharp blue slacks he had worn were in a corner, next to Aunt Pearl's box of dusting rags. They were shredded. He put on a pair of clean cotton pants, and the blue tennis shirt with the little alligator on the pocket that Mrs. Elversen had given him for Christmas. He slipped on the black loafers that Jeff had outgrown. Cousin Jeff. Be hearing enough about him tomorrow.

He let himself out of the apartment quietly, so quietly that he surprised two drug addicts fumbling in the hall toilet. They looked up, startled, then saw it was only Alfred, and went back to their spoons and needles. For a moment he thought they were lucky, they'd be getting out of the world for a while, but then he remembered all the old-looking, sick junkies he saw on the streets, hunched-up, desperate for a fix.

"Major and Sonny been lookin' for you," said a little boy on the stoop. Alfred nodded, trying to look cool.

He went a few blocks out of his way so he could walk down an avenue where he knew he wouldn't meet Major. There were big cats there that even Major was afraid of, out to get him for something or other.

The cars were still cruising, guys with their Saturday night girls, guys looking for Saturday night girls. Live music floated out of an upstairs apartment, and there was a burst of laughter. Alfred jammed his hands into his pockets and walked faster. Half a dozen boys his age lounged on a corner, and one of them called to him. He just put his head down and walked on. Couples strolled by, arm in arm.

He looked up once, and saw Henry across the street, dragging his bad leg and smiling as if being crippled was the best thing in the world. Probably coming back from the gym, thought Alfred. Maybe tonight Mr. Donatelli let him wash the fighters' socks. Then he remembered that Henry had brought him home, and he dropped to his knees behind a parked car. When passersby stared at him, he pretended he was searching for a lost coin. He waited until Henry had turned the corner. He didn't feel like thanking anyone for anything tonight.

He crossed the street and started down a block he hardly ever walked on, a block of low apartment buildings, a store-front church, a delicatessen, a pawn shop, and on the corner, a bar. Above the bar, on a dusty plate-glass window, were the faded letters, DR. ARTHUR COREY, DENTIST. Above that, on a dustier window, in even more faded letters, DONATELLI'S GYM. A light was burning.

He stood on the corner for a long time, looking up at the dim light until his neck hurt and his eyes watered. A jukebox was blaring through the open door of the bar, but he barely heard it. DONATELLI'S GYM. The door leading up to the dentist's office and the gym was sagging off its hinges, half-open. Beyond it was darkness. DONATELLI'S GYM. Joe Louis had worked out there once. He remembered his father talking about how he had gone over to watch. Maybe Sugar Ray Robinson, too. They weren't no slaves, and they didn't have to bust into anybody's grocery store. They made it, they got to be somebody. He thought about going into the darkness, up to the dim light on the third floor. Maybe if James was around, we could both . . .

He turned to walk away and saw the familiar, muscular figure moving toward him with that rolling swagger. Major! Wildly, Alfred bolted across the street, side-stepping a taxicab by inches, ignoring the horns and curses of braking drivers. On the other side he glanced over his shoulder, and stopped. It wasn't Major after all.

Slave. Always gonna be running, Alfred? And running alone?

He waited until the light turned green for him, and he strode back across the street, up to the door. A quivering chill ran up his legs, and his teeth began to grind and a ball of ice formed in the pit of his stomach and he took a breath and plunged through the door, into the darkness, a choking, musty darkness that stank of stale wine and antiseptic and sweat and urine and liniment. He hit the first step, feeling it sag under him, but he kept going, up wooden steps worn so smooth his loafers slipped backwards, but the chilly legs were getting warmer now. Put one after another, Alfred, panting, huffing, low steps but hundreds of them, thousands of them in the darkness, the stairs so steep he sometimes fell to all fours, scrambling higher, past the sign, DR. COREY, past the sign, GYM–THIRD FLOOR, faster until his breath tangled in his ribs, higher until his throat was dry, faster, higher, until a door loomed before him. GYM.

A faint light leaked through a crack, and he hurled himself up at it, paused, took another breath, and plunged into a large, murky room.

"Yeah?" A short, stocky man with crew-cut white hair looked up. His pale face was smooth and hard.

"I . . . I'm . . . I'm Alfred Brooks," he said, gasping. "I come . . . to be . . . a fighter."

The stocky man did not smile, or change his expression.

"Okay, Alfred Brooks," he said. "Take off your shirt."

21

CHAPTER 3

Donatelli circled slowly around him, his hand on his square chin, as if he were inspecting a slab of meat in a butcher store. He grabbed one of Alfred's hands, studying first the knuckles, then the palms.

"Big hands, you'll grow some more," he said. His voice was cold and rasping. He pointed at a battered white medical scale against a wall. "Get on."

Donatelli adjusted the vertical measure and fingered the sliding weights. "Five feet seven and three-quarter inches. One hundred twenty-four and a half pounds." There was no expression in his voice. He pointed at two wooden folding chairs facing each other. "Sit down."

Numbly, Alfred lowered himself to the edge of one chair, clutching his shirt in his hands. Donatelli sat down in the other, resting his heavy forearms on his neatly pressed gray slacks. His pale blue eyes flicked over Alfred's face and body. Alfred's eyes dropped down to the man's shoes, planted solidly on the wooden floor, black shoes curling with age but highly polished.

"Who sent you?"

"Nobody."

"Did you come by yourself?"

"Yes."

The pale blue eyes worked their way down to Alfred's hands, twisting and wringing the tennis shirt.

"Are you frightened?"

"Me? No, not—"

"A man must have some fear," said Donatelli, "and learn to control it, to make it work for him. Do you understand?"

Alfred nodded.

"Have you ever boxed?"

"No."

"I can see you've been fighting in the street."

Donatelli stood up and marched across the room, his square, boxlike body erect. He pulled a string dangling from the ceiling, and a dozen naked bulbs flooded the large room with pools of yellow light. In the center of the room was a boxing ring, its white canvas floor stained and lumpy. Donatelli leaned against four black-taped ropes, and turned his bulldog face to Alfred.

"There's no place to hide in a boxing ring. You're all alone in there with another man who wants to hit you more times, and harder, than you hit him. There are rules, and there's a referee to make sure you follow them. It's not the street. You follow me?"

"Yes."

Donatelli nodded, his bushy white eyebrows arching

over the cold eyes. "Sometimes kids come up here and they want to get in that ring right away and knock somebody's head off. No chance. You have to earn your way in there, you have to work hard for it. Most of the kids leave."

He straightened up and the ropes quivered back into place. One square, thick hand waved at a corner of the room. A gray, canvas bag, as large as a loaded army duffel bag, hung from the ceiling on a long chain.

"The heavy bag. Go on over and hit it. Not too hard."

Alfred walked across the room, the naked skin of his chest prickling. He punched the bag with his left fist. His knuckles burned and a sharp current of pain ran through his wrist, up his arm, exploding in his shoulder. The bag barely swayed.

"Over there," said Donatelli, pointing to another corner. A brown leather bag, not much larger than a paper lunch sack, hung from a swivel mounted on a round board screwed to the wall. "The peanut bag. Hit it a few times."

Alfred punched with his right, and the bag slapped against the round board. He missed with his left.

"The heavy bag is for power, to build up your arms and shoulders. The peanut bag is for speed and timing. Before you can go into the ring you have to be able to slam that heavy bag around all day and make that peanut bag sound like a machine gun."

"I could try," said Alfred.

"Thousands of kids can do it. Doesn't mean anything. The bag doesn't have any arms to hit you back with. You understand?"

"Yes."

"Let me tell you what it's like." He walked toward Alfred until they were standing face to face. His square head settled down into the crisp collar of his open-throated, short-sleeved white shirt. He had almost no neck.

"You get up at five-thirty in the morning, before the gas fumes foul the air, and you run in the park. That's to build up your legs and wind. You run smooth and easy, a little faster and a little longer each day. You run every day, rain or snow, unless you're too sick. Then you go home and eat breakfast. Juice, two boiled eggs, toast, and tea. You go to school?"

"I work."

"You don't eat too much lunch, it just makes you slow and tired. No fried foods, no beans, no cabbage, no pies and cakes, no soda. After work you come to the gym. Jump rope, stretching exercises, sit-ups, push-ups, deep-knee bends. You do them until you can't do any more, then you start all over again. You go home, have a good dinner. Meat, green vegetable, fresh salad, milk, fruit. You're asleep by nine o'clock."

Donatelli strolled beside the dusty plate-glass window. Neon signs blinked on and off in the street below, throwing pink, green, and blue mists against his smooth-shaven cheeks. His thin lips barely moved as he talked.

25

"You'll do it for a week, maybe two. You'll feel a little better physically, but all your friends, your family, will say you're a fool. You'll see other people smoking and drinking and staying out late, eating anything they want, and you'll start to think you're a fool, too. You'll say to yourself, 'All this sacrifice, and I'll probably never even get to be a good fighter.' And you'll be right, nine times out of ten."

His voice was lower as he moved away from the window and walked along a green wall, looking at the rusting clothes lockers and the faded posters advertising old prizefights.

"People will try to drag you down. Some will laugh at you for wanting to be a fighter. And others will tell you you're so good you don't need to train, to go to bed early. How far did you go in school?"

"Eleventh grade."

"What happened?"

"I quit."

"Why?"

"Didn't seem like any reason to stay."

"What makes you think you won't quit here too?"

Alfred swallowed. He suddenly wished he hadn't come up the steps, that he was somewhere else, anywhere. He thought of the cave.

"Well?"

"I want to be somebody."

"Everybody is somebody."

"Somebody special. A champion."

Donatelli's thin lips tightened. "Everybody wants to be a champion. That's not enough. You have to start by wanting to be a contender, the man coming up, the man who knows there's a good chance he'll never get to the top, the man who's willing to sweat and bleed to get up as high as his legs and his brains and his heart will take him. That must sound corny to you."

"No."

"It's the climbing that makes the man. Getting to the top is an extra reward."

"I want to try."

Donatelli shrugged. "Boxing is a dying sport. People aren't much interested anymore. They want easy things like television, bowling, car rides. Get yourself a good job. Finish high school. Go at night if you have to."

"I'll try hard."

"Talk it over with your parents."

"I don't have any. I live with my aunt."

The pale blue eyes came around again. They seemed softer now. But the voice was still cold and flat. "It's not easy trying to become a contender. It's never any fun in the beginning. It's hard work, you'll want to quit at least once every day. If you quit before you really try, that's worse than never starting at all. And nothing's promised you, nothing's ever promised you."

He reached up and pulled the string. The room was murky again, except for the single light bulb. Donatelli spoke from the shadows.

"I'm always here, Alfred. I live here now. Whatever

you decide, good luck to you." His footsteps echoed in the darkness as he walked away.

Alfred left. He moved carefully down the steps. They were still narrow and slippery, but no longer darkly threatening. He was halfway home before he realized that the twisted tennis shirt was still in his hand.

CHAPTER 4

"The white man's got his foot on your throat," roared the shaven-skulled man on the stepladder. "You gonna lick his shoe?"

"Noooo, brother," chanted the street-corner crowd.

"He shoots you down in the street. You gonna keep turning the other cheek?"

"Hell-o, that's tellin' it."

Aunt Pearl sailed serenely past the nationalist rally, the three girls clustered around her like starched white tugboats escorting a blue cotton ocean liner. She looked neither right nor left, eyes focused straight ahead, her face glowing with the quiet joys of Sunday, her day. Alfred trailed a few steps behind, a strange new excitement bubbling in his stomach. He had hardly slept, the time in Donatelli's gym running through his mind all night, like a movie. But he felt more awake than he usually did on Sunday morning, and the streets seemed more alive than ever before.

The nationalist on the stepladder, his quick hands

slashing through the air, was whipping his growing audience out of its morning listlessness.

"You gonna keep beggin' Whitey for crumbs off his table?"

"No."

"You gonna . . . Well, look at that." His forefinger stabbed out toward Alfred. "Ain't that sweet? On his way to pray to Whitey's God, learn to Tom and turn the other cheek. . . ."

Alfred hurried on, away from the crowd's nervous laughter, past young men leaning against padlocked shop doors, tapping their shiny shoes and nodding their heads to silent music. He pushed through chattering families, past cool Ivy-League types and their light-skinned girl friends. He had almost caught up to his aunt's bobbing white hat when someone yelled, "Brooksy, hey Brooksy."

A stocky boy with horn-rimmed glasses came out of a crowd of young people lining up at the corner. He had a thick sheaf of leaflets under his arm. Alfred pretended he hadn't heard him, a big-shot politician he had never liked in high school.

"Come on with us, Brooksy, we're having a march," he said, grabbing Alfred's sleeve.

"Can't," said Alfred. "I'm going to church."

"We need you, man, come on," he said. Alfred shook his arm free. "Come on, we have to wake our people up, things are happening, man."

"Maybe later," said Alfred, starting to edge away as a slim girl joined the boy. "Not now."

"Now," she said firmly. "We want our rights now, and you can be part of this. . . ."

"Save your breath, Lynn," said the boy. "Can't you see that Alfred Brooks is a happy little darky."

"Harold," snapped Lynn, "that's no way to get new . . ."

Alfred moved on, faster, angry at the sudden sting in his eyes, the sudden emptiness in his stomach. He brushed past the outstretched hand of a wino and caught up to his aunt and cousins. The serene look on Aunt Pearl's face calmed him at first, then made him angrier. Sometimes you'd think she was deaf, dumb, and blind, he thought.

The little store-front church was only half filled when they walked in, but Reverend Price was already behind the lectern, thumbing through his Bible. His wife, Sister Lucille, was in her tall wooden chair on one side of the pulpit. Aunt Pearl took her place up front with the choir, and the girls picked up their tambourines and sat in metal folding chairs behind her. Alfred took a chair toward the rear.

He tried to slide into his soft, dreamy Sunday morning trance, but it didn't come even when the hymns began and Aunt Pearl's pure, sweet voice rose above the others, filling the little room with a sound like golden honey. The other members of the congregation turned to watch her, as they always did, and most of them were smiling.

Reverend Price began to speak in his deep, heavy voice, the words booming out like beats on a muffled drum. Sister Lucille waved her arms, leading the congregation in the response.

". . . Amen, preacher, say it again," they chanted.

Somebody poked Alfred in the ribs. He turned. A man sitting near him pointed toward the back door. Alfred twisted around in his seat.

Major was standing in the doorway, his muscular hands clamped to his wide leather belt. Behind him Hollis was grinning, his big teeth hanging out over his lower lip. Alfred turned away quickly. The back of his neck began to itch and burn. He tried not to, but he had to turn around again. They were gone.

Services had never seemed so long, the metal chairs never seemed to have so many digging edges. He forced himself to listen to the sermon just to blot out the picture of Major and Hollis.

". . . The devil's agents wear new uniforms these trying days, but their poisons are the same. They say go out and hate the white man. They say go set yourself down in places where you are not wanted. They say . . ."

Alfred let the words wash over him. Devil's agents. What did they look like? Shaven skulls maybe, or big muscles. That pretty girl, Lynn, at the march. Was she a devil's agent? He'd have to ask James. James would roll his eyes that comical way he had and say, Alfred, my man, if she's a devil's agent I'm gonna go right down and apply for a . . . James. In jail now, maybe thinking I put him there. Pray they don't beat him too bad.

The morning services finally ended. The children turned their tambourines upside down and took the collection. Aunt Pearl was the last one out, telling the Reverend how much she enjoyed his sermon, how sad she was at having to miss his afternoon teachings. She probably is, thought Alfred.

The subway ride out to Jamaica took more than an hour. Aunt Pearl kept her eyes closed, as if she were still in prayer, except when Charlene, Sandra, and Paula got restless and started giggling among themselves. Then she opened her eyes and scowled them into silence. It was hot in the subway car. Big black fans turned slowly on the ceiling, moving the hot air around and spinning off bits of soot. The splintery wicker of the subway seat pressed through his damp pants.

A pretty girl his age came aboard wearing a fresh-looking pink dress, and sat opposite him. Her skin was smooth and cocoa-colored, and she stared right back at him through oversized sunglasses. Alfred looked away first, wishing something would happen, the train would get stuck between stations, the girl would fall down and need help, anything so he could walk over, suave and sophisticated, "I'm Alfred Brooks, may I be of service?" —just like in the movies.

But the train reached Jamaica without any trouble, and their bus was waiting at the corner. They rode past grimy little factories and projects and, after a while, along clean, grassy streets lined with neat little houses.

Aunt Pearl was always so proud that one of her sisters married a man with a good job who bought her a house in Queens. Just before they got off the bus, Aunt Pearl leaned over and whispered, "Lord help me, Alfred, but I told Dorothy and Wilson on the phone how you fell off that stone fence. Be no need to say nothing else."

Aunt Dorothy, tall and bony, was waiting at the front door with her own small daughter, Diane. She hugged the three little girls and Aunt Pearl, then hooked her arm into Alfred's, kissed him on the cheek, and pulled him inside. Uncle Wilson, tall and bony, too, loped across the front room and dropped a big hand on Alfred's shoulder. "You're getting taller, boy, you're gonna be big as Jeff one of these days."

They sat down to eat right away—cold chicken, thick slices of ham and cheese, potato salad, macaroni salad, bread, plenty of lemonade, a seven-layer cake. Uncle Wilson, Alfred, and the four girls dug in, but Pearl and Dorothy, acting as if they didn't talk on the phone at least twice a week, chattered away, picking daintily at their food. Afterwards the girls ran upstairs to Diane's room, and Aunt Dorothy and Aunt Pearl cleared the table and went into the kitchen. Alfred followed his uncle out to the back porch and watched him carefully fill his pipe and light it. The afternoon sun made shadows on his uncle's bony face, deepening the hollows under his cheekbones. Wilson rocked in his chair and pointed his pipe stem at Alfred.

"Still at the grocery store?"

"Yes."

"Like it there?"

"It's all right."

"Opportunity for advancement?"

Alfred shrugged.

"You got to be thinking ahead, Alfred. World is changing, opening up for colored people." He sucked on his pipe, staring out at a row of purple flowers.

"Yes, sir, Alfred, world is changing. Me, I never was past the county line until the war came. Now your cousin Jeff's been all over the country. Talkin' about joining the Peace Corps after college, go to Africa. Got a letter from him the other day, says he's going to be ready when the opportunities come." Uncle Wilson smiled into the cloud of smoke rising from his pipe, and he crossed his bony legs.

"Been thinking about your future, Alfred?"

"Some."

"The trades is opening up. Electricians, carpenters, bricklayers make good money these days. They'll be more places for colored people soon. But you have to be ready, have to have your education. Have to be qualified. You think about the trades at all?"

"Sometimes."

"Jeff says he might go into law, maybe teaching. He's going South this summer, work in those voter registration schools. Says once colored people are all voting the—what's he call it?—yeah, the white power structure going to find more jobs for them, more opportunities for advancement. World is changing."

They lapsed into silence, Wilson comparing his pipe

clouds, Alfred slouching in the porch chair. He could hear the girls giggling upstairs, and the chatter of the women in the kitchen. He tried to remember Jeff. He must be nineteen or twenty now, very tall, taller than his father and bigger across the chest and shoulders. He had only seen Jeff a few times in the last three years since he went away to college. But he always heard about Jeff, winning all the prizes at high school graduation, a scholarship to college. And he had to look at all the pictures—Jeff in a tuxedo at his freshman prom, Jeff being sworn in as president of his sophomore class, Jeff shaking hands with somebody important. He sank deeper into the chair, feeling all the good food lying heavily on his stomach.

Wilson rocked and smoked, and after a while they talked about the Yankees and how the Mets' pitching was perking up. Alfred felt better then. It was peaceful out here. Uncle Wilson and his pipe seemed so strong and wise. For one wild moment he wanted to tell him about Mr. Donatelli, but he swallowed it back and the moment passed. The light began to fade, and Dorothy called them in for more cake and lemonade, and then it was time to calm down the girls, who were cranky, say good-bye, and start back to Harlem.

"You think about the trades, Alfred," said Uncle Wilson, and then the bus came.

Aunt Pearl and the girls dozed on the subway, but Alfred wasn't tired. He watched a huge black man, drunk and bleeding from a cut on his head, sprawl out in the

36

middle of the car and go to sleep. Twice, when the train lurched, he sat up, looking around fiercely. Alfred tensed, wondering how he could stop the man if he went crazy and attacked Aunt Pearl or the girls. But each time, the man lay down, smiling sweetly, and went back to sleep.

The streets seemed dirtier when they got out, and the apartment seemed smaller. It always happened after visiting in Queens. Alfred helped Aunt Pearl open the couch and put the girls to sleep. Then they sat down in the kitchen and drank some milk.

"What's troubling you, Alfred?"

"What made you ask that?"

"You been so quiet. You thinking about James?"

"Some."

"You want to talk about it?"

"Not right now."

"When you do, honey, you know you can always talk to me." She kissed him on the forehead and went into her bedroom.

Alfred unfolded his bed, and sat down on the edge, staring at the green-painted plaster beginning to crack over the kitchen sink. A roach scurried over the cabinet, paused, then scurried back into the wall. There was a scuffling noise out in the hall. The addicts.

Tomorrow was Monday, blue Monday, dirty Monday. The store would be filthy, there would be dozens of cartons and cans to stack. Opportunity for advancement? Sure, they might even let me deliver on the bicycle. He saw Major shuffle along the clubroom floor. Uncle Alfred. The Epsteins would be asking about the attempted robbery. About James. He would scratch his head and play dumb, like you always do when the white man asks those questions you better not answer. He's got his foot on your throat, you gonna lick his shoe? Come march with us, Alfred. Maybe later. Happy little darky. World is opening up for colored people. Devil's got new uniforms. We'll get you. Everybody wants to be a champion, Alfred. Slave. Nothing's promised you. Slave. Opportunity for advancement? You have to start by wanting to be a contender.

He stood up quietly, and tiptoed into his aunt's room. She was snoring. He took the alarm clock from her bureau and put it on the kitchen cabinet. He stared at it for a long time before he set it for five-thirty. Then he snapped off the light. He kept waking up through the night, listening for the tick, staring at the glowing hands. Had he set it right, was it wound up enough, was the alarm button pulled out?

The last time he looked at the clock it was quarter to four, and the faintest tinge of pink was brushing the window.

CHAPTER 5

The grass was spongy with dew and the air was cool and sweet, filling his lungs until they pressed against his ribs and a stitch ran up and down his side. Then he was crunching over gravel. The sky was blood-red. It was going to be another warm day but not yet. He couldn't help smiling, he'd sing if he had the breath. He was all alone in the park. The birds were chattering in the overhanging trees, sitting on their stoops telling all the bird gossip. Smooth and easy, Alfred, build up the wind and the legs, smooth and easy, pick up those feet. The breeze streamed past his cheeks, cooling, and the muscles of his legs stretched and got warm and his elbows swung along his sides and the silly smile grew wider and he thought he'd burst from the joy of . . .

"Hold it right there."

Two policemen stepped out from behind a bush, and the birds stopped their chatter.

"Where you going this time of morning?"

"I'm running."

"I can see that," said the smaller cop. "Where you running to?"

"Just running, officer. I'm in training."

"For what?" asked the bigger cop.

"Boxing," said Alfred.

The two policemen looked at each other, and the little one winked. "Oh, yeah, I know you. Fighting for the heavyweight championship of the world next week, right?"

Alfred shook his head. His mouth suddenly felt dry and gritty and his tongue thick. "Just starting."

"Who's your manager?"

"Mr. Donatelli."

The big cop nodded. "I've heard of him. Had three champions, two at the same time, I think. What's your name, boy?"

"Alfred Brooks."

"Okay, Al, you keep training. We'll look for your picture in the papers." They laughed and disappeared back into the bushes.

The spring was out of his step, and suddenly the stitch seemed unbearable, and he could hear cars moving through the park. Gas fumes. That's enough for today, he thought, knowing it wasn't, and he slowed down again and started trudging back to the apartment. The good feeling was gone. His sneakers felt heavy, as if they were filled with water.

Aunt Pearl was bustling around the kitchen, getting the girls ready for school when he came in.

"Alfred. Where you been? Are you just getting in now? You been out all night?"

"Took a walk."

"A walk?"

Sandra saved him, screaming that Paula had hidden her hair ribbons. Aunt Pearl got busy quieting them down, feeding them breakfast, helping Charlene make the lunch sandwiches. When the girls finally left for school, Aunt Pearl turned back to Alfred, her eyebrows raised.

"Now. Where you been?"

"Just went out. Couldn't sleep."

"Where you been you need the alarm clock?"

"Took a walk."

"You said that already, Alfred. You look at me now. Are you in trouble?"

"No."

Her voice dropped to a whisper. "Somebody after you for something?"

"No."

"I ain't gonna press you, Alfred, you do a man's work and I ain't gonna treat you like a boy. But I know something's wrong. We eat all right, don't we?"

"Yes."

"We ain't on welfare, the rent's paid up, we got nice Sunday clothes. We're doin' all right. Did your Uncle Wilson get you all upset?"

"Uncle Wilson?"

"I heard him braggin' about Jeff. You do all right too. You got a job, you . . ."

"Big job."

"Alfred! You be glad you're workin'. Streets are full of men hangin' around, waitin' for trouble."

"I'm gonna be somebody," he said, feeling his throat tighten up again.

She surrounded him with her soft arms. "You some-body right now, Alfred. A good, God-fearing boy, minds his aunt, helps . . ."

"Somebody special," he said, pulling away.

She dropped her arms and took a step back, peering up into his face. "How you mean, Alfred?"

He shrugged. "Some way."

"Alfred," she whispered, "you wasn't really fixin' to go with James that night . . . Alfred!"

She was still calling his name as he ran out the door.

Lou Epstein, the oldest, shortest, and baldest of the three Epstein brothers, barely looked up from the cash register when Alfred entered the store.

"I want to talk to you," he said.

He signaled to Jake, the middle brother, to take over the cash register. He led Alfred back to the storeroom. Ben, the youngest brother, was licking a black crayon and marking prices on soap-flake boxes when they walked in. Lou jerked his bald head, and Ben left the room.

"Some boys tried to break into the store Friday night. You hear about it?"

"No."

"That friend of yours, James Mosely. The police caught him. Put him in jail over the weekend."

42

There was a long silence, and Alfred studied the green vegetable stains on Lou's apron. "What are they going to do with him?"

"They'll let him go on probation. First offense, and nothing was stolen. You didn't even hear about it?"

"I heard something."

"You heard something." Lou rubbed his pale scalp. "You heard maybe who the other boys were?"

Alfred shook his head and lowered his eyes to Lou's shoes. They were worn and cracked, with holes for Lou's bunions.

"You're a good boy, Alfred, we all think you're a good boy. I told the police not to bother you. But sometimes it's hard to . . . well, we trust you, but for your own sake there's no point tempting fate. You understand."

Alfred shook his head again, and Lou shrugged his thin shoulders. "We'll see, we'll see. Okay. After you get done sweeping up, help Ben with the new crates." He went back to the cash register.

They said very little through the morning. Jake kept shooting glances at Alfred out of the corner of his eye. Even Ben was quiet, Ben who always asked Alfred how he had spent his weekend, and then winked knowingly when Alfred said he had seen some movies, watched television, and hung around. There was tension in the store, as thick and heavy as the air before a rainstorm. Aunt Pearl sensed it too, when she came in on her way to work. She didn't say anything about Alfred's leaving without breakfast or forgetting his lunch. She just put the paper bag on the counter and walked out, frowning.

43

He ate in the back of the store, alone, chewing sandwiches that tasted like cardboard in his dry mouth. The Epsteins always let him take soda or milk and a piece of fruit. But today he felt too uncomfortable to pick out the rest of his lunch.

The afternoon was hot. Flies buzzed in through the door, landing on the open watermelons and the sweet corn, climbing up the sweating pickle barrel. Two heavy-set white men, perspiring through their summer suits, came in and whispered with Jake and Lou. They looked like detectives to Alfred. One of them wrote something in a black leather notebook, nodded, and snapped it shut.

"We'll stay in touch, Lou. Bet you're glad now you took our advice on that new alarm."

There was plenty of work to do, and he could pretend to concentrate hard on peeling the rotten leaves off the cabbages or sponging the spilt milk from the refrigerator floor. He was arranging the fruit in the front window, half-watching Lonny, the sixty-year-old delivery boy, park his bicycle, when he first saw James. The round face, swollen and grim, was framed between hand-printed window signs advertising the week's special sales.

"Hey," Alfred called, starting toward the door. He stopped at the cold, hard look in James' eyes. James turned and swaggered away. Like Major.

At quarter to three, Lou Epstein banged open the lower cash drawer and counted the big bills into a brown envelope. Alfred went to the back to wash his hands while Lou filled out the deposit slip. When he came out, Jake was stuffing the envelope into a pocket. Sure, thought Alfred, now I understand about no point tempting fate. They don't even trust me to go to the bank anymore.

There was little to do in the late afternoon. Alfred swept and reswept the dark wooden floor just to keep moving, his head down, avoiding the Epsteins' sad, distrustful looks. He kept remembering how good he had felt in the park, jogging over the gravel, the wind in his face, his muscles heating up. Hold it right there, said the cop. He kept seeing James' face on the wooden floor, cold eyes in a swollen face.

He swept his way into the back room, jamming the straw broom into nooks and crannies he had already swept clean. The tiny wires of the new burglar alarm snaked along the molding of the back door, and for an instant he thought of sweeping them loose, one good, hard swipe should do it. Come back at night, get in the back . . . Wait until next Friday when there would be a lot of money in the register. . . . Come back with James, then he'd know I didn't purposely let him walk into a trap. He swept his way out among the shelves. Can't do it. Maybe never be able to do anything but sweep up this crummy store.

Nothing's promised you, that's what Mr. Donatelli said. Why'd I have to go up there, listen to all that foolishness, get excited about it like a little kid? Glad no-

45

body but those cops saw me running this morning, that was foolishness, too. Hold it right there, said the cop. Slave, said Major. Good boy, said Lou.

Alfred felt in his pocket. Enough for a nice dark movie, he thought, sit and watch it forever.

"Hey, Alfred."

He looked up, startled. "Henry."

"What time you comin' by?"

"Where?" He stared at the ever-grinning face peering in through the door.

"The gym."

"Gym?"

"Yeah. Mr. Donatelli said you was up Saturday night. He asked me about you."

"What you tell him—"

"Gotta run. See you later."

"Henry." But he was gone.

CHAPTER 6

He bounced up the steps two at a time, friendly old steps, trying not to grin like a fool because Mr. Donatelli would give him that blue-eyed once-over and you better look tough and all-business on day number one. He hit the door and stepped in, and his jaw dropped. The gym looked like Reverend Price's Hell.

Half-naked bodies were jumping and twisting and jerking around, bells rang, the peanut bag went *rackety-rackety-rackety*, ropes swish-slapped against the squeaking floorboards, someone screamed, "TIME," gasping voices, "Uh . . . uh . . . uh-uh," and an enormous black belly rushed past, spraying sweat like a lawn sprinkler. Alfred shrank back against the door.

Slowly he picked out objects he had seen before. The heavy bag was swinging wildly on its chain as the boy with the enormous belly battered it with fists as big as cantaloupes. The peanut bag was rattling against the round board as a skinny white boy with hunched shoulders beat it into a brown blur. Near the medical scale, two Puerto Ricans were jabbing at their reflections in full-length mirrors. They were quick as cats. Other boys were jumping rope, jerking up and down like mechanical jacks-in-the-box, or straining on leather floor mats until their neck cords popped, or slamming medicine balls into each other's stomachs. In the ring, their heads encased by black leather guards, two fighters danced around each other, ducking, bobbing, bouncing on and off the quivering ropes. A stick-thin old black man with white hair was yelling at them, "Faster, faster, pick it up."

The room began to shrink, and the noise pounded against Alfred's head. He looked around for Mr. Donatelli or Henry, but neither was in the room. He saw an old sign on the wall.

Amateurs—$2 weekly

Professionals—$5 weekly

PAYABLE IN ADVANCE

He felt for his wallet. There would be at least two dollars in it, but there was no one around to take his money or tell him what to do. No one was even looking at him. Leave now, he thought, come back some other time, when it's less crowded, when Henry's around. But something told him if he left now he would never come back. He waited, watching the thin man unstrap the fighters' headguards and shake a black pencil of a finger in their faces. He watched the enormous belly move lightly across the room toward the peanut bag, and take over when the skinny white boy dropped his arms and shuffled away. The Puerto Ricans climbed into the ring, and the rope jumpers began shadowboxing. Everyone seemed to know what to do. Some other time, he thought, edging backwards out the door, turning so quickly that he never saw the chubby little man until his elbow banged into a soft chest.

"Uhh."

"Oh, I'm sorry, I—"

The little man held up a small hand. "That's an illegal punch."

"I didn't mean to—"

"If the referee saw that you'd lose the round. Automatically." He was smiling, his reddish cheeks puffed out like a squirrel's.

"I wasn't looking."

"No harm done. Your first day?"

"Yes, Mr. Donatelli said—"

"He's not here today, one of his boys has a fight at the Garden tonight."

"I'll come back some other—"

"Today's better than tomorrow. What's your name?"

"Alfred Brooks."

"I'm Dr. Corey."

"The dentist downstairs?"

"Aha. Alertness." The little red face moved closer, and tiny gray eyes blinked behind thick spectacles. "For that I will offer you a pearl of wisdom. Are you ready?"

"Yes," said Alfred, feeling his jaw relax.

"The stomach is more important than the chin. Hit the chin and you may break your hand. Kill the belly and the head will die. Do you read me?"

"I don't think so."

The dentist shrugged. "I am too far ahead of my time. Start with sit-ups, Alfred. Make your stomach like a rock." Huffing slightly, he walked over to the ring. The thin man smiled and patted him on the shoulder.

Alfred walked over to the floor mats. Two boys, in gym clothes and boxing shoes, were balancing themselves on their shoulders, kicking their legs up in the air. One was the skinny white boy, the other was a well-built Negro with light skin and reddish hair. Alfred waited until they finished the exercise before he lowered himself to a corner of a mat.

"You gon' work out in street clothes?" asked the redhead.

"All I got," said Alfred.

"Let any trash in nowadays," he grumbled, rolling over and starting push-ups.

Alfred stretched out on his back, putting his hands under his head and pointing his toes. He jerked up fast, went back down, and jerked up fast again. In high school gym class he had always been good at sit-ups.

"What you call them?" asked the redhead.

50

"Sit-ups."

"Haw. You hear that, Denny? He calls them sit-ups." The redhead laughed and poked the white boy.

"So show him how to do it, Red," said Denny, looking annoyed.

"Don't waste my time with trash," said Red, getting up and walking away.

"Let me show you," said Denny, rolling over on his back. The scrawny body came up very slowly, quivering with the strain, folding over until the face and the knees were almost touching. Then Denny went back down again, even more slowly.

"Thanks," said Alfred.

"You bet," said Denny.

Alfred tried it, coming up slowly, inch by inch, fighting to keep his legs straight and his heels on the mat as his shoulders began to quiver and the muscles in his stomach tightened painfully. Up and then over, toward his knees, feeling the long muscles in his thighs pull and his back muscles tear, until the blood flooded his head and he couldn't go any further. Then slowly back down again, his body shuddering, till slowly, gently, he lowered the back of his head to the mat. He took a deep breath, and the pain faded away.

"That right?" he asked, but Denny was already on the other side of the room, skipping rope.

The second sit-up was harder than the first, and the third was harder still. But by the fourth his muscles began to get warm, like a car engine heating up on a cold morning, and they stopped struggling against each other. He did twenty sit-ups before he fell back exhausted. Not bad, he thought, been such a long time. He sat up and looked around. Dr. Corey and the thin man were talking at ringside. Boxers were grunting away all over the gym. No Henry.

He turned over and started on push-ups, slowly, concentrating on keeping his body straight. After thirty-four push-ups his arms felt rubbery.

"Hey, Alfred, been here long?" Henry dragged up, a box under his arm. "Had to go downtown, pick up something for Bud."

"Who's Bud?"

"Bud Martin, Mr. Donatelli's assistant," said Henry, pointing at the thin man. "See you later."

"Hey, Henry."

"Yeah?" Henry turned impatiently.

Alfred tried to think of something to say, anything to keep Henry from leaving. His eyes fell on the sign. "Do I have to pay my two dollars now?"

"No. When you can spare it easy. If you can't pay, Mr. Donatelli won't throw you out."

"Henry," called Bud Martin.

"Right there."

Alfred did a few more sit-ups, but the sweat running under his street clothes began to itch. Some of the boxers were weighing themselves, and joking, and drifting off into the shower room behind the rusty lockers. The gym was quieting down. The peanut bag was silent. Dr.

Corey passed him on the way out, but didn't look down. Henry was over in a corner, helping Bud Martin pack a black satchel. Alfred was alone again. He felt another urge to leave, but he forced himself to stroll over toward Henry and Bud, his hands in his pockets, casual, so no one could tell he felt out of place.

Up close, Alfred could see Bud Martin's ribs pushing through his tattered T-shirt. But the bony hands were sure and quick as the old man stuffed small jars and rolls of tape into the valise.

"Hey, Bud," shouted Red, shouldering past Alfred.

Bud didn't look up. "Need some more cotton tips, Henry."

"Sure." Henry disappeared back into the dressing room.

"I'm talkin' to you, Bud," said Red.

"Talk," snapped Bud.

"I need my hands taped."

"You learn to do it yourself."

"Willie Streeter don't have to do it himself."

Bud looked up, his black eyes hard in the skull face. Muscles all over his face twitched underneath the drum-tight skin when he talked. "But Willie knows how, and there's a difference right there."

Red mumbled something and walked away, again brushing Alfred.

"Some people," said Bud, "think this is a nursery school. Henry?"

"I got the cotton tips," said Henry, putting a cello-

53

phane package in Bud's hand.

"Better bring me another jar of Vaseline."

"Right."

"Always use a lot of Vaseline on Willie's face," said Bud, talking mostly into the black satchel. "He's got dry skin that cuts so easy. Sometimes even the grease don't help."

"What happens if he gets cut?" asked Alfred.

Bud reached into the satchel and pulled out a small jar of yellowish paste. "Stops the bleeding, keeps the cut clean."

"What is it?"

"Clarence Martin's Magical Potion. Patent Pending."

"What's in it?"

Bud winked. "I got doctors call me from California ask what's in it."

"Do you tell them?"

"You crazy, boy? Only Donatelli and me knows what's in it, and even he don't know exactly how much of each special ingredient I use."

"Like a trade secret?"

"Exactly." Bud grinned, showing pink, toothless gums. "I invented it forty-one years ago. Had this lightweight, skin so thin would start bleeding if his mother kissed him. Lightning Lou Epp, real good little—"

"I need a headguard," said Red.

"I'll get it," said Henry, limping up with the Vaseline jar.

"Stay where you're at, Henry," said Bud. "Now, what

you need a headguard for?"

"Gon' spar."

"You know the rules, boy. No sparring unless the boss or me is watching. He's not here, and I ain't got time."

"Don't be an old woman," said Red.

"If you don't know the rules maybe you don't belong here."

"I pay my dues. I belong here more than a lot of people."

"Rules the same for everybody," said Bud.

"Just get me a headguard."

The room fell quiet. Whoever had started punching the peanut bag stopped, letting it squeak into silence on the swivel. The Puerto Rican boys, Denny, the enormous belly, the others, moved into a circle around Alfred, Henry, Red, and Bud.

"Ever since you come," said Bud softly, looking into the satchel, "you been a smart meat. Be sweet, boy. Joe Louis been up here and he had a good word for everybody. Sugar Ray and Cassius Clay been up and treated everyone fine."

"Skip the lip," said Red. "Your job's to get me a headguard when I want it."

"My job's to help Mr. Donatelli train you how to fight. But you got to get to be a man on your own."

"You saying I ain't a man, you old crow?" Red's hands came up. Alfred saw they were taped.

"You wanna fight somebody you fight me," said the enormous belly, pushing Alfred out of his way. "I say you ain't no man, neither."

"Mind your business, Jelly Belly," said Bud. Carefully, he took the Vaseline jar from Henry's outstretched hand and placed it in the satchel. He snapped the satchel shut, and looked up.

"Now. What's your problem, boy?"

Red leaned forward, his skin flushing with sudden blood. Bud's gaunt face seemed to get blacker.

"If you had any teeth I'd knock 'em out," said Red.

"Go make believe I got teeth."

Red's right hand balled into a fist, and the arm shot out like a jackhammer, straight at Bud's mouth. The old man never blinked, lazily waving his left arm, knocking Red's hand aside. One skinny black hand whipped out and cracked against Red's jaw.

Red backed up, tears springing to his eyes. Alfred suddenly felt sorry for him. Red ran to his locker, pulled out his clothes, and bolted out of the gym.

Bud looked around. "Don't nobody tell the boss about this. Everybody gets a second chance around here. Now go on with what you were doin'. Show's over."

The others drifted away, and Bud fingered the lock on the satchel. "Nobody ever said it was easy. Got to come up here, day after day, got to put out, and some days nobody even looks at you 'cept to say you're doin' something wrong."

He locked the satchel. "That's part of it. You hungry enough, you keep at it." He looked right at Alfred. "You Alfred Brooks?"

"Yes."

"Figured. Tonight you gonna see a real fight, no slappin'."

"Me?"

"Yeah. Henry's got your ticket. The boss said if you ever came back you might as well see what you came back for."

CHAPTER 7

Hundreds of people milled under the marquee of Madison Square Garden as Alfred and Henry came up from the subway. Seedy men with mashed-in faces waved their cigars at tall, well-dressed businessmen carrying attaché cases. Big, rough teen-agers jostled through the crowd, their sleeves rolled high enough to show off blue and red tattoos. Young white girls with piles of golden hair hung on the arms of flashily dressed men. Alfred's nose tingled. The smells of perfume and after-shave lotion and mustard and beer were mixed together. The sharpest of all were the big-time Harlem gamblers in white dinner jackets, elegantly stepping with glittering women who looked as though they posed for the advertisements in *Ebony* magazine.

"C'mon, Alfred," said Henry, pulling his sleeve.

At the ticket window, a fat-faced white man scowled down at them, and Alfred was sure he would tell them to get lost. But Henry said, "Mr. Donatelli left two for Henry Johnson," and a little white envelope slid out between the bars.

The man who took their tickets at the door scowled, and Alfred was sure he wouldn't let them in, but he tore the tickets without a word and returned the stubs. Then he turned to scowl at a white couple right behind them. The usher scowled, and the man selling programs scowled, and the man behind the frankfurter stand scowled, and the guard who checked their tickets at the black curtain scowled, and then they were inside the Garden.

Alfred caught his breath. It was huge. It was almost a circle, and the seats rose right up the walls toward a ceiling of cables and beams. In the center of the floor, gleaming white under hundreds of spotlights, was the ring. The ropes were wrapped in red velvet.

"Keep movin'." Someone stepped on the back of his shoe, and Alfred stumbled on. Three more scowling men, in blue uniforms, pointed them on until they reached their seats—attached wooden chairs on the arena floor ten rows away from the ring.

A dignified little man in a bright blue tuxedo climbed through the ropes and pulled down a microphone from the tangle of wires and blazing lights over the ring. He asked them all to please rise for the national anthem. The music swelled out of an organ and boomed through the half-empty arena, sending little shivers up Alfred's spine.

"Hey, brothers, how's it goin'?" Jelly Belly plopped into a seat next to Henry, his great stomach bouncing under a pink sport shirt. He peered over at Alfred. "You

59

the one nearly got caught in the middle of that thing to-day? Yeah, didn't recognize you in the Sunday suit."

Self-consciously, Alfred began to loosen his tie, but Jelly Belly tapped his hand. "Don't, brother, we need a little class around here."

"Did you see Willie?" asked Henry.

"Just came from him," said Jelly Belly.

"How is he?"

"He's Willie, y'know what I mean? Mr. Donatelli's in there, telling him just how to fight Becker and Willie is nodding his head and everybody knows, sure as hunger, Willie's gonna go in there and do it *his* way."

"I read in the paper coming down here," said Alfred, "that Willie Streeter could be the next champion."

"Mr. Donatelli's counting on it," said Henry.

Jelly Belly bounced up. "Chow time. Anybody want a hot dog?" He waved at one of the hot dog vendors.

"Hey, Jelly," said Henry, "you know Mr. Donatelli said you gotta cut down on all that—"

"You lightweights gotta worry about the pounds," said Jelly, winking at Alfred, "but us heavies need to keep up our strength."

The preliminary bouts were a blur of bodies and punches for Alfred, but he jumped up every time Henry and Jelly did. He nodded when Jelly poked him and said, "Some hook Chico's got, huh?", and he tried to look knowing when Henry yelled, "Y'ever see footwork like that, Alfred?"

He tried to follow the action, but he kept thinking

about the day he and James found the boxing and wrestling magazine on the street. They flipped right past the boxing section to the wrestling pictures. James decided they should become professional wrestlers, and he made up their names. Mosely of the Jungle and Bad Brooks. When they got back to Alfred's stoop, James started jumping up and down, pounding on his chunky chest and howling so loud people leaned out of their windows to watch.'Alfred fell off the stoop laughing, and James ran down and put a foot on his stomach. An old lady stared at them, and James growled, "That's how Mosely of the Jungle triumphs. They all die laughing." Alfred tried to push the thought away and concentrate on the fights.

"Here we go," said Henry.

Mr. Donatelli, solid and square, moved down the aisle, clearing a path for Willie Streeter, a tall, handsome Negro who waved to the crowd. He wore a white robe with his name on the back. Bud Martin and Dr. Corey were right behind him. The crowd started cheering and clapping even before Willie slipped gracefully through the ropes into the ring, and sat down on a three-legged stool. He sat there quietly, as Donatelli whispered in his ear and Dr. Corey and Bud knelt to massage his arms and legs. The three older men were wearing long-sleeved white sweaters with WILLIE STREETER written across the back in red letters.

The ring announcer pulled the microphone down again. "Ladeeez . . . and gentlemen. A ten-round bout. In this corner, wearing black trunks and weighing one hundred seventy-four pounds, from Houston, Texas . . . Junius Becker."

There was some polite applause and a few boos. Half a dozen people sitting together near ringside cheered for Becker.

"And in this corner, in white trunks"—the crowd began to cheer loudly and steadily—"weighing one hundred seventy-four and one-half pounds, from New York City . . . Willie Streeter."

The cheering and the applause grew as Willie stood up. He smiled and waved a red glove at the crowd. So cool, thought Alfred. So confident. He settled back to watch Willie beat up poor old Junius.

The first few rounds were slow. Willie and Junius were circling, throwing out punches that were easy to duck or knock away. Henry was squirming in his seat, "Stick him, Willie, keep him off balance."

Jelly, his voice becoming shrill, shouted, "Move in on 'im, Willie, please, Willie."

Between the rounds, Willie nodded as Donatelli whispered in his ear. Alfred tried to imagine himself up there, taking a long drink of water from the taped-up bottle in Bud's hand, spitting it out in one long stream into a bucket, opening his mouth so Dr. Corey could jam in the white mouthpiece.

The bell rang, and both fighters rushed together, Willie's left arm pumping out like a machine, slamming into Becker's face, rocking him backward against the red velvet ropes.

"Keep on 'im, Willie, don't let him rest," shrieked Jelly.

Henry shouted, "Stick, stick . . . Look at him, Alfred, he's . . ."

Whatever Henry said next was swallowed in the crowd's roar as the two fighters smashed into each other, banging heads and stumbling backwards. Becker fell to one knee, his gloves on the canvas floor.

The referee began counting, "One . . . two . . . three . . ." Becker shook his head, as if to clear it. ". . . four . . . five . . . six . . ." Then he climbed to his feet. ". . . seven . . . eight." The referee wiped Becker's gloves on his gray shirt and stepped aside, signaling the two men to continue boxing.

Suddenly the crowd went, "Ooooohhhhh," and Jelly leaned toward Alfred. "He's hurt."

Willie was bleeding. It looked like a deep cut to Alfred, right on the outside corner of Willie's left eye.

"Willie's in trouble," said Jelly.

Alfred saw it immediately. Becker was aiming his punches at the bleeding eye, and all the fight seemed to be draining out of Willie. He wasn't attacking anymore, he was just dancing backwards, his gloves up in front of his face. Becker rushed in, punching away at the unprotected belly. All Willie's coolness and confidence seemed to be gone.

At the end of the round, Donatelli, Bud, and Dr. Corey swarmed over Willie. Bud moved in with a gob of yellowish paste on the tip of his finger, but the manager waved it away. He peered at the cut eye and called over the referee. Suddenly, the crowd was booing and Junius Becker was waving his arms and Willie Streeter was trying to struggle away from Bud and the dentist.

"What happened?" asked Alfred.

"Technical knockout, TKO," said Henry. "Mr. Donatelli had the fight stopped."

The crowd continued to boo as Donatelli and Bud each grabbed one of Willie's arms and dragged him down the ring steps and up the aisle.

Jelly jumped up. "Come on," he said.

It took them fifteen minutes to work their way through the crowd, even with Jelly's belly leading the way. On all sides the booing rose, and a man cupped flabby hands around his mouth and yelled, "Ya sissy, I cut myself worse shaving every morning."

They finally entered a long, dim tunnel. A big guard stood cross-armed in front of a closed door.

"Sorry, fellas, you can't come . . . Oh, Jelly, how are ya?" He unlocked the door and waved them into a large room, bare except for some benches and old lockers. Willie was sitting on an upholstered table, clenching and unclenching his taped hands as a doctor worked on his eye. Donatelli was whispering to him, and Bud and Dr. Corey were shaking their heads. Two men with State Athletic Commission badges on their jackets were staring up at the ceiling. The only other person in the room, a husky young man with a broken nose, came over to Jelly, his hand outstretched.

"My man Spoon," said Jelly, grabbing the hand. "What's the mood?"

"Not good," whispered Spoon, loosening his tie from his button-down collar.

"How's Willie taking it?"

"We'll see in a minute."

The doctor put a strip of white adhesive tape over Willie's cut, and left. Willie touched it, tapped it, blinked his eye, and whirled on Donatelli. "I woulda won and you know it, I woulda won that fight, I woulda . . ."

The manager's face reddened, and it seemed to Alfred that he swallowed down something he was about to say.

"Look, Willie, do you want to go through life with one eye, for one lousy fight?"

"Nothing wrong with my eye," yelled Willie, as Donatelli, his mouth a slit, turned away. "You can't even look at me after what you did, throwin' in the towel like that."

"Talk about it tomorrow," said Donatelli.

"Right now," yelled Willie, jumping off the table. His eyes swept his audience, all looking at their shoes. "If you're scared of a little blood, I can get a manager who isn't."

"Go right ahead," said Donatelli.

"You watch your mouth," growled Bud, grabbing Willie's arm. "After what you did in there tonight you oughta be down on your knees to that man, give you a way to save your gutless damn face—"

"Bud, leave him alone," said Donatelli.

"No chance, Vito," said Bud. Willie tried to jerk his arm loose, but the thin fingers tightened. "You never did know the difference between pain and injury, did you, Willie, you was always so—"

"Leave him alone," said Donatelli. He looked very tired.

Spoon raised his eyebrows at Jelly, who nodded and gently pushed Alfred and Henry toward the door. "We better go."

Out in the corridor, the guard touched Jelly's shoulder. "What's going on in there?"

"Nothing much."

"What's all the yelling?"

"Very painful stitches," said Spoon, his dark face expressionless.

"Oh."

The four of them walked toward a red exit sign. Spoon was shaking his head. "Too bad. Mr. Donatelli was really counting on Willie to go all the way."

"But it's just one defeat," said Henry.

"More than that," said Jelly. "Willie showed some dog tonight."

"Dog?" asked Alfred.

"It's true," said Spoon, stopping. "It was a bad cut, but if Willie had forgotten about it and kept pressing Becker he would have won, he might even have knocked him out in that round. But he got scared, it was the first time he had ever gotten hurt, really hurt, and he got scared. The way he concentrated on protecting that eye left him wide open, and Becker was sure to hurt him somewhere else. Mr. Donatelli saw that and stopped the fight, to save him from being hurt and to save him, I think, from showing himself a coward in front of the crowd. I can't think of another manager who would have done that."

"Me either," said Jelly. He grinned. "Same old Spoon. You're still giving lectures."

Spoon smiled and opened the exit door. "Sometimes I forget I'm not in front of a classroom."

A crowd of older men stood in front of the Garden, arguing about the fight. A workman on a ladder was pulling Willie Streeter's name off the marquee, letter by letter.

"I'm driving uptown," said Spoon. "Can I give anyone a lift?"

"Thanks," said Jelly, "but I got a girl friend lives around the corner and I promised to do her a favor tonight. She goes to cook and baker's school and I'm gonna check her homework."

"Same old Jelly Belly."

"I'm a growing boy, Spoon. I think these guys are going uptown. You know Henry Johnson, and this is a new tiger comin' around the gym. I don't even know his name."

"Alfred Brooks."

"Hi, I'm Bill Witherspoon." He shook hands with

Henry and Alfred, and tapped the front of Jelly's pink shirt. "School's out in a few days, Horace. I'm coming up to the gym and see if I can whip some of that belly off you."

"All muscle," said Jelly. "Be good, men."

Spoon's car was an old blue Plymouth, and the three of them squeezed into the front. The back seat was covered with papers and books.

"Sorry you're so crowded," he said, moving the car into traffic, "but I'm studying for my permanent teacher's license and I've been collecting every scrap of paper I can get my hands on." He stopped for a light, and looked at Alfred. "Do you want to be a fighter?"

"I'm going to try," said Alfred. The light changed and Spoon looked away. Alfred watched the street lights play on Spoon's face. There were thin scars around his eyebrows, and two crossed blue scars on the bridge of his battered nose. "I saw your name on a fight poster up in the gym."

"Did you?" Spoon smiled out at the traffic. "For a while I was rated the Number Seven light-heavyweight contender."

Alfred leaned forward. "How come you quit?"

"It was very simple. One day, Mr. Donatelli said, 'Billy, I think it's time.' That's all he said. 'Billy, I think it's time.'"

"Why was that?"

"I was beginning to take too much punishment. I was winning, but I was starting to get hit regularly. This

68

thing," he touched his nose, "was a big part of it. I argued, of course, but there isn't much point arguing with the boss unless you're right and he's just testing you. He told me he felt I should go back to college, full-time. I had taken a few courses at night. I had the money he made me save while I was going good, and I still had my eyesight and my hearing and my brain in one piece. I graduated from City College and I started substitute teaching. Last year I married a teacher. Mr. Donatelli was the best man." Spoon shrugged. "There I go, another speech. You fellows better tell me where to turn."

They rode the rest of the way in silence, Spoon driving carefully as the clean, well-kept buildings in the quiet white neighborhoods gave way to shabby houses on streets filled with black children and garbage. Once Henry whispered something to him, but Alfred let it go by—he was too busy winning the championship of the world, doing everything Mr. Donatelli told him to, never getting hurt or in trouble, smiling modestly down at Jelly and Spoon and Bud and Dr. Corey as the referee raised his arm.

"It's a long road, Alfred."

"Huh?" The car was parked in front of Henry's house, and Spoon was smiling at him.

"It's all right. I still have daydreams about what might have been." Spoon offered his hand. "Nice meeting you, Alfred, and seeing you again, Henry."

"You'll be coming up the gym?" asked Alfred.

"I'll be there. Good night."

"Good night. Thanks for the ride."

The car pulled away, and Henry tugged at his sleeve. "Want to sit on the stoop for a while?"

"I got to run tomorrow."

"Oh, yeah, that's right. Well, take it easy."

"Yeah."

Alfred took a few steps, then turned. "Henry?"

"Yeah?"

"Henry, I want to . . . uh, well, thanks a lot, Henry, you and your father too, for carrying me home that night."

Henry's thin face beamed. "Oh, sure, man, that's all right. You got KO'd, right? Can't win 'em all."

"Thanks."

He walked fast, in a hurry to get into bed and play the whole day back in his mind. The policemen on the corner raised their eyebrows at him, smiling and nodding like that, and the people on the stoop he waved to looked at each other, but Joe Louis had a good word for everybody and Sugar Ray and Cassius were men enough to be sweet. He started to say hello to the three boys standing in front of his stoop, but the word died in his throat when they turned around.

"Where you been, Uncle Alfred? We been waiting up all night for you," said Hollis.

"Now, let's us take a little walk," said Major, grabbing his arm.

CHAPTER 8

"**M**onday night and dressed so fine," said Major, leaning against the locked clubroom door.

"So fine," echoed Sonny, circling behind Alfred.

"Where you been, Uncle Alfred?"

Alfred stared at his black shoes. His knees were quivering. He wished he were sitting down.

Hollis showed his buck teeth. "You know Uncle Alfred can't talk 'less James is around to tell him what to say."

"Where's James?" asked Alfred.

" 'Where's James, where's James?' " mimicked Major.

"What you want with me?"

" 'What you want with me?' " mimicked Hollis.

"I'll tell you," snapped Major, pushing away from the door with his elbows. "Friday night we gonna hit Epsteins' again, only this time we're goin' in easy. This time, you gonna help us."

"No chance," said Alfred. The words were out of his mouth before he could swallow them back.

"What you say?" Major's eyes narrowed. "What you say to me?"

Alfred jammed his hands into his pockets, and pressed his fingers through the cloth into his thighs. His knees stopped quivering. "I said no."

"You said no?"

Alfred tensed for Major's attack, but there was only surprise on the heavy face.

"Look, slave, you don't have to come with us."

"No."

"All you got to do is disconnect them wires on the burglar alarm."

"No."

"Whatsa matter with you?" said Hollis.

"We'll split with you," said Major, "and you don't even have to come."

A vein popped out on Major's forehead, and his thick arms shook from the strain of keeping his muscles flexed. Where was all that coolness, that confidence? "No chance at all," Alfred said.

"You crazy?" asked Hollis, looking from Alfred to Major, then back to Alfred. "What's got to you?"

"I gotta go now," said Alfred, quivering again as he took a step toward the door.

Major jumped in front of him. "Where you think you going?"

"Home."

"Not till I let you." The knife came out fast and clicked open. "You ever hear of a squealer's scar?"

"Yeah."

"Then you know what I'm gonna do. One cut, from your mouth to your ear. You wear it the rest of your life."

Hollis was frozen, his mouth hanging slack. Sonny's eyes were dull and staring. Alfred pressed down on his toes to quiet his knees.

"You want the scar?"

"No."

"Then you're gonna do it, right?"

"No."

Major's tongue flicked out between his lips, and a bead of sweat broke out on his nose. "No?"

"He's crazy, Alfred's crazy, man," said Hollis.

"Must be crazy," said Major, straightening out of his knife-fighter's crouch. "I'll give you to Wednesday to get back to your senses."

"Answer's no," said Alfred.

"Don't have to decide now."

"I've decided now."

Major's voice was almost a scream. "But why?"

"Because I don't need to, that's why," said Alfred, taking a second step toward the door.

"The Epsteins don't care about you, you just a black nigger slave to them."

"Maybe so."

"Just a black boy to carry out their garbage, that's all."

"Got nothin' to do with them," said Alfred, moving past Major.

"You scared."

"You think that if you want." He put his foot on the first step.

"Why?"

He reached the door and unlocked it. "I got things to do, that's why."

"You got to Thursday to decide," screamed Major. "You got to Thursday—"

Alfred closed the door behind him just as his knees sagged, shuddering violently. Then he straightened, and all the way home he wanted to raise his right arm to the ringside crowd on the stoops.

CHAPTER 9

The birds were gossiping in the trees. There goes Alfred, smooth and easy, watch his knees come high and steady, cham-peen Alfred, looka him.

"Hang in there, Al, you're lookin' good," yelled the smaller cop, and Alfred waved back and put on a burst of speed just to show them how good he could look, his arms swinging easily at his sides, sucking in the air through his nostrils, letting it out his mouth. He ran for more than an hour, over grass and gravel, until the sun burned away the early mist and dried the dew. Squirrels skittered out of his way. Twice he saw other runners, and they waved and smiled at him. Like they were all partners. A stitch chewed at his side, but he kept running until the stitch disappeared. His breath caught in his ribs, but he kept running until he got his second wind. He didn't stop until cars and buses began to snarl and belch their way through the roads of the park, filling his nose and mouth with gas and oil fumes.

On the way home, he stopped every twenty steps for

two quick deep-knee bends. He tried to hop up the first flight of stairs on his left leg and the second on his right. He almost made it.

At the door, he touched his toes ten times before throwing it open and striding smack into Aunt Pearl.

"Alfred?" Her face was stern, her hands on her hips.

"Yes, ma'am." He winked at the girls, kissed his aunt on top of her head, and cakewalked around the kitchen table. "No applause, folks, please."

"You drunk?"

"Now, Aunt Pearl, you know I never drink till after breakfast."

Charlene giggled in her cereal.

"Where you been?"

"Out running."

"From what?"

"From One Hundred Tenth to Eighty-fifth Street and back, nearly three miles."

"Don't you make fun of me, Alfred. Wipe that smirk off your face. Where you been?"

"Ladeez . . . and, uh, ladies. An announcement." The twins began to giggle too. "Introducing Alfred Brooks, the up-and-coming champeen of the world."

"Now you gonna be the down-and-out chump if you keep on." She snatched up a big wooden serving spoon. "You ain't that big I can't still whip that smirk off your face."

The girls ducked back into their cereal.

"Now. Where you been?"

"I been running in the park, build up my wind, get in shape, strengthen my legs—"

"Slow down. What are you talking about?"

"Aunt Pearl, I'm gonna be a boxer."

"Boxer!" The word rattled the cereal bowls, and the girls came up with milk on their noses. "Are you out of your mind? Boxer! Now you better . . . Alfred Brooks, I can tell, you're not fooling, are you?"

"No, ma'am. Mr. Donatelli. At the gym. He's gonna teach me to—"

"Boxer! And get your head busted open? What would your sweet momma say, Lord rest her soul, if she knew I let you . . ." Her voice trailed off. "Where you go last night?"

"Madison Square Garden."

"With who?"

"Henry and—"

"Henry Johnson?"

"Yeah. And Jelly Belly and Spoon—"

"Spoon?"

"Bill Witherspoon. He's a schoolteacher, used to be a boxer."

"Hmm." A trace of a smile tugged at the corners of her mouth. "An' I been so worried. First you get beat up, then act so strange yesterday morning. Then out so late last night and your good suit's all wrinkled, I thought you had some more trouble. An' this morning you sound like you're drunk or something."

"I feel good."

"Who's this Mr. Donatelli?"

"He's a boxing manager and he has a gym. Henry works there. He's had a couple champions."

"You planning to quit your job for this thing?"

"Not right away. Be a while before I get to be professional."

"I don't like this boxing business one bit. Full of gangsters, and people get hurt bad."

"Mr. Donatelli's no gangster. Last night he made Willie Streeter stop 'cause he had a cut eye, and he made Spoon quit 'cause he was getting hit too much. And Spoon was winning fights."

"We'll talk to Reverend Price about this. Now let's eat."

"I'll have orange juice, two boiled eggs, toast, and tea."

"You'll have what? This ain't a restaurant."

"Boxers can make big money, Aunt Pearl. You might not have to work no more, buy you a little house by Aunt Dorothy's, a car so you can drive to church on Sunday, a—"

"Don't you load no promises on your head, honey."

"I'm serious, Aunt Pearl."

"I know you are. You never been excited about anything in your life till today. But I just wish it was something else."

CHAPTER 10

L eft . . . left . . . snap it out, Alfred, . . . left . . . right . . . right . . . left . . . left-left . . .

The first week was all pain, steel claws ripping at his shoulder muscles, raking his arms. The sweat rolled off his forehead and flooded his eyes, but they wouldn't let him stop to brush the sweat away . . . left . . . left . . . snap it out . . . even as his reflection grew hazy in the full-length mirror. Keep punching, they yelled, faster, harder, more.

"Your arms hurt, Alfred?"

"A little, Mr. Donatelli."

"They should hurt a lot. Okay, now. Time."

Time . . . time . . . three minutes of shadowboxing, one minute of rest, three minutes of shadowboxing, one minute of rest, time . . . time . . . until he woke up moaning one night, his arms as heavy as cement sacks, his fingers numb. Charlene was at the foot of the bed. She looked scared.

"Should I wake up Momma, Alfred?"

"No. Go on back to sleep. I had a bad dream."

"It musta been terrible."

Left . . . left . . . right . . . left . . . harder, harder, faster . . . snap it out, left . . . right . . . c'mon, c'mon . . .

The second week was worse. Bud yelled at him to stay up on the balls of his feet and Donatelli told him to keep his chin tucked against his chest.

Even Dr. Corey had his two cents worth: "Never take your eye off the peanut bag, Alfred."

Sit-ups, push-ups, deep-knee bends. Angel and Jose, the Puerto Rican boys, cackled like hens when the medicine ball knocked him over like a tenpin. Denny grinned and threw it again harder, but Alfred was braced and ready. It only staggered him.

He could barely lift his arms up to his locker after workouts. Twice that week he fell asleep before dinner. At dawn, the alarm clock buzzed him awake like an angry rattlesnake.

That Sunday, after the morning service, Aunt Pearl marched him up to Reverend Price. She told him that Alfred needed guidance. He didn't like the way the Reverend looked down at him, scratching his big jaw, as if he were a school kid. But somewhere deep in his aching muscles a tiny voice was praying that Reverend Price would make him quit.

"What seems to be our problem, Sister Conway? Has Alfred strayed from the path of righteousness?"

"He's boxing, Reverend, he's—"

"Oh," said the preacher, his eyes moving around the room, his voice getting vague. "Youth is a time of great physical energy, Sister, and of curiosity. This is a passing phase. He'll soon grow tired of this meaningless pursuit and devote his . . ."

Left . . . left . . . faster, faster . . . atta boy . . . pick it up . . . chin in . . . right . . . right . . . snap it out . . .

By the middle of the third week the pain began to fade. He rushed through his exercises just to get in front of that mirror and shoot out those jabs, straight out, hard, until the little shocks in his shoulder told him the punches were straight and true. Spoon came up that week, and they all watched him spar a few rounds with the heavyweights, Jelly and Pete Krakover. Dr. Corey said that Spoon looked better than Willie Streeter did that night at the Garden.

Spoon worked with Alfred on the heavy bag, showing him how to keep his wrist straight but relaxed so he could hit hard without hurting himself. But Spoon worked with Angel and Jose too, and there were some days when no one looked at him but Henry.

He started waking up before the alarm that week, fresher in the morning, stronger. The hour in the park was the best time of the day. It sometimes seemed as if he could run forever, showing his heels to the friendly policemen, waving at other runners. He wished he had someone to run with, someone like James, a partner, pacing him over the wet grass and over the gravel, sprinting across the deserted roadways, dropping back into a jog on the dirt paths. He'd even slow down for James. Someday, he thought, old James would come out from behind a tree, howling like Mosely of the Jungle, and he'd wink at Bad Brooks and fall into step. They had seen a movie like that once, two cowboy brothers who had a fight, and at the end they joined up again, riding into town together to face the gang. They won too.

The thought would make Alfred sad, and he'd speed up until he pushed it out of his mind. Henry was the nearest he had to a partner now, and Henry would never know how good it could feel when a running wind chilled the sweat in your hair.

At breakfast, Aunt Pearl would make some comment about his huge appetite eating them out into the street, but she smiled when she said it. And then he went to work. Jake was still going to the bank in the afternoons, but Alfred couldn't get bothered about it, not when he felt his muscles flex every time he stacked the canned goods or lifted a box. Even the worst part of the job, carrying out the loaded garbage cans, didn't seem so bad when the muscles across his back and shoulders rippled and tensed. They had always rippled and tensed, but now even lugging garbage cans was part of training, of getting into shape.

There was a lull one afternoon. There were no customers in the store, and Alfred began throwing the hook at his reflection on the door of the steel food locker. He had just knocked out Jose, Angel, and Denny, one, two, three, when old Lou wandered into the back room.

"What's this, Alfred?"

"Sorry, Mr. Epstein, I was just—"

"From the shoulder it has to come, the power is here." He tapped a bony shoulder, shuffled his feet, and threw a slow but graceful left hook. "You want to be a boxer?"

"Yes. I'm training at Donatelli's gym."

"A good man, Donatelli. Ask him about Lou Epstein someday."

"Hey! Are you Lightning Lou Epp?"

"How did you know?"

"Bud Martin talked about you. He said you were real good, but you cut too easy."

A slow smile spread across Lou's thin face. "He remembered, eh? A good cut man, Bud Martin, one of the best. How long you been training?"

"About three weeks."

"Forget it. I would tell my own son the same thing, especially my own son. Forget it."

"Why?"

Lou sat down on a packing case. He rubbed a small red sore on the top of his bald head. "Why? I'll tell you, Alfred. Once it was something, boxing. There were dozens of fight clubs in the city. You could see a good fight every night of the week. Irish fighters, Italian, Jewish fighters, then Negro fighters, there were enough matches for anybody who wanted to fight. No more.

Even a good fighter can't make a living out of it. You know why?"

"People aren't interested in going to fights?"

"Part of it," said Lou. "Television came in, and used the same fighters over and over again, a few got rich, the rest had to get jobs. And even the rich ones lost their money. The racketeers, the crooked matchmakers, the rotten managers just—"

"Mr. Donatelli's not like that, he—"

"Sure, sure," said Lou, raising a spidery hand. "Donatelli's one in a million. That's why he has to sleep in a room by the gym. Boxing people don't like to do business with an honest man. And another thing, the kids these days aren't interested in learning to fight. It's hard work. Nobody wants to work no more. Who knows, maybe they're right."

He stood up. "You see that friend of yours, James Mosely, anymore?"

"Not since . . . not for a long time."

"Okay. You tell Bud hello for me, Donatelli, too."

Off your heels . . . faster . . . left, right, left, right . . . snap it out, jab, hook, jab . . . harder . . .

He began to lose track of the days. They rolled off like perspiration, up at dawn, run, breakfast, work, the gym, home, dinner, television, sleep. Sometimes on Fridays or Saturdays he went to the movies with Henry and Jelly, but it wasn't like going to the movies with James. Henry just sat there, his mouth open, staring at the screen, and Jelly was always jumping up for candy

84

or ice cream. Not like the old days when Alfred would follow James up to a corner of the balcony and root for the monster and cheer the Indians and afterward change the ending of the picture if they didn't like how it came out.

In late July, Aunt Pearl went to the Elversen's summer house and left the girls in Queens with Dorothy and Wilson. The apartment seemed large and empty. Now he could sleep late on Sundays. Sometimes he slept right through the day, getting up only to eat and doze in front of the television set.

Then Monday and dawn and the alarm clock.

The peanut bag was easy, once he got the rhythm he could stand under it all day, making it sound like a machine gun. Henry would watch him, grinning, as if he was really doing something, but Donatelli would walk by without even looking. Alfred could hear the manager think. The bag doesn't have any arms to hit you back with.

"Real good speed on the bag, Alfred," said Henry.

"Anybody can do that," said Alfred.

Henry looked away.

Left . . . left . . . hook, shift, hook, jab, right . . .

"Open your mouth," said Dr. Corey one day, shoving in a white plastic mouthpiece. "When you're ready for your first fight, I'll make you a custom-fitted one."

"Aaaargh." Alfred gagged and spat it out. Jelly slapped his knee, and Denny laughed.

"Again," said Dr. Corey.

"I can't breathe."

"You'll have to breathe through your nose."

"Quick, sharp breaths," said Spoon. "In, out, in, out, that's the way."

He gagged for half an hour, but then he got it, and went back to the mirror, up on the balls of his feet, quick little steps, forward on the jab, sideways for the hook, da-da-dum-dum, quick and easy.

"Time," called Donatelli, passing by. "Your foot-work's coming along, but this is no dancing class. Snap that jab out, harder . . . harder . . ."

And when the workout was over and every muscle shrieked, there was nothing like standing under the shower, the hot water drowning all the ache, closing your eyes and tilting your face up into it.

"Whaddya, drinking it, Alfred? C'mon, there are five guys out here waiting to get in."

He ran into Major one night as he was coming home from the gym.

"Hey, Alfred, how you been?"

"Okay."

"Don't run off, man, wait a minute. We never see you 'round the clubroom no more."

"Been busy."

"Yeah, I heard you're working out. Say, man, you're not still sore about that little misunderstanding we had. I was just trying you out."

"Sure."

"Well, come around," said Major.

"Sure."

"I mean it. James comes by once in a—"

"James around?" said Alfred.

"Sometimes. I'll let you know."

"Do that."

Willie Streeter came back to the gym, sullen and overweight. Donatelli took him to a training camp in the mountains for ten days to try to get him in shape for an out-of-town fight. The temperature in the gym sometimes reached 101 degrees and everyone started snapping at each other. One day, Pete Krakover threw a boxing shoe at Jelly.

"Use your own trunks, fat meat."

Jelly looked up from the locker bench, his body slick with sweat, his mouth sucking air like a fish's gill.

"What?"

"You heard me, fat meat. Use your own damn trunks."

"What I want with your stinking Polack trunks?"

"You black tub a lard," yelled Pete, rushing forward on floppy shower clogs. Jelly stood up to meet him, hands up.

Jose and Angel danced between them, a step ahead of Bud Martin.

"He no wear your trunks, Petey," yelled Angel.

"He too fat," yelled Jose.

"I sent 'em all out to be washed," said Bud.

Pete grinned sheepishly. "Sorry, Jelly."

"The heat, man," said Jelly, plopping back down. "You ain't used to it. Always snows in Poland."

"I never been there," said Pete. "My grandmother says it's beautiful in the summer, green and warm."

"No kidding?"

Snap it out . . . snap it out . . . snap it out . . .

"Time," called Henry. "You're just pushing that jab, Alfred, you got to throw it."

"Why don't you try?" snarled Alfred. "I'm sorry, Henry, I didn't mean it."

"That's okay," said Henry. "Time."

Time, time, time, thought Alfred, flicking out the jab. I can do this in my sleep. Across the gym, Spoon and Bud were watching Angel and Jose spar in the ring. They were both turning pro soon. Jelly and Pete were waiting to go in next. He looked up at the weight chart over the scale. Six weeks, six damn weeks, gained six pounds and never punched anybody except my own face in the mirror. I'm not even an amateur yet.

"Time," said Henry. "What's the matter, Alfred?"

"Nothing's the matter."

"You sure?"

"Sure."

"Okay. Time."

Donatelli came back on a Friday, his thin lips tight. Willie had lost his out-of-town fight. The manager spent the afternoon leaning on the ring ropes, watching Jose and Angel spar. Alfred threw out his jab mechanically, staring at the back of the square, white-topped head,

88

willing it to turn around and look at him. The head didn't move.

"Hey, man, you're looking sharp," said Major, swaggering into mirror view.

"Let's go, snap it out," said Henry.

"Got any fights comin' up, man?"

"C'mon, Alfred, keep punching, left . . . left . . ."

Alfred dropped his arms and turned around. "No, I'm just—"

Bud Martin tapped Major on the shoulder. "That boy's working. You can talk to him later, outside." He jerked a thumb toward the door.

"Okay, baby," said Major. "Come on around, Alfred. Little party tonight. James gonna be up."

He swaggered across the gym, rolling his big shoulders, stopping only to rap the peanut bag on his way out.

"You and Major tight now?" asked Henry.

"No."

"Wonder what he wants."

"Just being friendly."

"I'll bet," said Henry. "Time."

He threw out his arms mechanically, left, right, left, right, but there were no shocks in his shoulders, just a dull ache along the ridge muscles of his back. Do this in my sleep, he thought.

"Time," said Donatelli. He shook his head. "You're not doing anything at all today, Alfred. You're not concentrating. Is anything the matter?"

"No."

"You've got to work harder."

"Yeah."

Donatelli nodded and strolled away, over to the heavy bag. He put one hand on Jelly's shoulder and one on Pete's and all three of them laughed at something Jelly said. Come on back here, thought Alfred, come on back. Show me something, tell me I'm gonna spar someday, put on a pair of real gloves.

"Time," said Henry.

"Time out," said Alfred. He walked to his locker, peeling off the wet gym clothes. Too hot today. Too damn hot.

He showered and dressed quickly. Henry was waiting for him at the door.

"You want to go to the movies tonight?"

"No."

"Triple feature, be fun. Jelly says if the monster don't win tonight he's gonna tear the movie house down."

"I said no."

"You going to the clubroom?"

"I don't know."

"You're in training, Alfred, you better not—"

"I can take care of myself."

He walked quickly down the steps, the long, steep, dirty steps. He wondered if Donatelli was just too cheap to fix them. A guy could break his neck.

The street was still hot, even with the sun sliding out of sight. Music blared out of open windows. Kids clattered up and down the gutter. Friday night. On every street corner people lounged and stared, waiting for something to happen. Cars cruised up and down. Men brought out the tables for cards and dominoes. Go home to an empty house, eat dinner, watch television, go to sleep early like every other night. Too hot to sleep, he thought. Sleep for what? To run tomorrow and shadow-box and count out your life in sit-ups?

He headed toward the clubroom. Wonder what James is doing these days. Never even called me back. Still mad about that burglar alarm. Straighten that out. Just drop in for a little while. See what's happening.

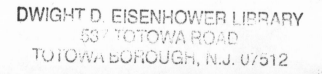
DWIGHT D. EISENHOWER LIBRARY
537 TOTOWA ROAD
TOTOWA BOROUGH, N.J. 07512

CHAPTER 11

Major saw him first. "There's the champ."

"Hey, champ," said Sonny.

"It's my main man, Alfred," said Major, throwing an arm around his shoulders and pulling him down into the darkened clubroom. "What's your drink, brother?"

"I'm in training," said Alfred. A single red bulb shone over the spinning record player. He squinted at the shadowy figures in the room, some dancing, others sprawled on floor pillows. "Where's James?"

"He'll be by. Wine?"

"No, thanks."

"Take a night off, man, you're in shape. Gotta have some kicks."

Major's girl, June, came out of the shadows. "You come alone, Alfred?"

"Yes."

"Good," she said, linking her arm in his. "Got somebody I want you to meet."

"Can't stay long."

"Wait till you meet her." She led him across the floor, weaving among the dancers, stepping over couples whispering and necking. She lit a match, and a dark, chubby girl with a curly, blond wig and thick, pink lipstick smiled up at Alfred.

"This is Arlene," said June. The match went out, and June let his arm go.

"I'm Alfred Brooks."

"Hi."

"Dance?"

He was surprised at how easily she came into his arms, so close that the strong, sweet smell of her perfume made him dizzy in the heat of the crowded room. The music was low, funky blues, and he swayed to it.

"You live near here?"

She shook her head, and the stiff hairs of the wig brushed his nose. "I'm visiting June. She's my cousin."

Major came around with the wine bottle, and Arlene drank from it. Alfred pushed it away, twice, when Major pressed it against his chest. Then he came back with half an orange soaked in vodka.

"This is good for you, man."

Why not, Alfred thought. He sucked on it, feeling new heat rise out of his empty stomach into his head. The party became a blur, a sweet, sticky blur. Major left the wine bottle with him, and Alfred and Arlene danced into a corner. Someone began pounding conga drums.

Hollis swam by, and punched his arm. "Good to see ya, Alfred."

"Yeah. James come in?"

"Not yet."

"You sure he's coming?"

Hollis patted a jacket pocket. "You can be sure he's coming."

"Who's James?" asked Arlene.

"A guy I know," said Alfred. "Let's sit down awhile."

Someone began passing a cigarette around, and the way everyone dragged on it he knew it was marijuana. Alfred shook his head when Arlene put it between his lips.

"It'll relax you, honey," she said, stroking the back of his neck, and he inhaled.

The red bulb burned out, and it was pitch-dark in the clubroom. The wine bottles kept coming around, and the cigarettes. Except for soft laughter, the music covered all sound in the room. Like a nice dark movie, he thought. He took longer pulls on the bottle, and deeper drags on the cigarette to keep the warm, soft feeling in his head. Once the door opened for some newcomers, and he saw Arlene smiling up at him, her face puffy, the blond wig tipped over one eye.

At dawn, an invisible fist slammed into his stomach, and he barely made it out to the alley. He leaned against a brick wall and tried to catch his breath. Newspaper pages fluttered along the street on a morning breeze. He saw a patch of pink sky between the buildings. For a moment he thought about the park, the good feeling of gravel underfoot and the wind streaming past his face. Then he went back down the basement steps.

Sonny had passed out on the couch, and Hollis' date was slumped over the mop sink. Hollis was dancing with Arlene. There was just a little bit of wine left, and they passed it around, trying to get the nighttime glow started in the dirty glare of rising daylight. Some new people came with bottles wrapped in brown paper bags, and Major blacked out the little basement window with his jacket. The party started all over again.

"Hey, Alfred," mumbled Major, pulling him away from Arlene. "Your man."

"James."

The round face was thin, the eyes sunken. His suit seemed too big for him.

"Where you been, James?"

"Lil Unca Alfid," said James. His teeth were yellow.

"Where you been, James?"

"I been 'round."

"Never called or nothing."

"What for?"

"We were partners, remember, we . . ." He felt dizzy, and shook his head. "James, I forgot about that burglar alarm. Honest. I didn't mean for you to—"

"It don't matter now."

"Does. Don't want you thinking—"

"I know you didn't mean nothing, you never mean nothing. You just fool enough to forget about that alarm." He turned his back on Alfred.

Major came over and put an arm around James' neck. "Hollis got something for you, brother."

The clubroom began to tilt for Alfred, but he took a

deep breath and grabbed the back of a chair. Hollis pulled a packet of white powder out of his jacket pocket. Alfred stumbled over.

"No, James, you don't wanna mess with that stuff, you don't wanna—"

"Go 'way, Unca Alfid." James was almost snarling.

"No good, James," mumbled Alfred, feeling the room sway.

James took the packet and began fumbling with it. Alfred followed him into a corner, trying to clear his head, steady himself. "You and me, James, partners."

"That was kid stuff," said James as his fingers, trembling, tore at the packet.

"Listen to me, James, please." Alfred leaned against the tilting wall, his legs buckling, his eyes fogging.

"What you got to say?" asked James, suddenly staring at Alfred, waiting as Alfred's lips moved without any sound.

He tried to clear his head, to think, to answer James' question, but the floor came up and sent him sprawling. James looked down at him, shook his head, and went back to his white powder.

CHAPTER 12

Far, far away, the rattlesnake was buzzing, short bursts, time to run, time to run, time, time, screamed Henry, but Jelly Belly was sitting on his head. Jose and Angel, chattering in Spanish, were jumping on his stomach. Mr. Donatelli was sitting on his legs shouting, shift your weight, shift your weight. Then they all disappeared and left him alone, lying on the linoleum kitchen floor in a pool of ice-cold sweat. The telephone was ringing. He crawled over to it and fumbled with the receiver. The phone crashed to the floor.

"Yeah?"

"Alfred?"

"Aunt Pearl?"

"You all right, Alfred? You sound so strange."

"All right."

"I can't hear you."

"Just woke up."

"It's nine-thirty, Alfred."

"Slept late."

"It's nine-thirty at night."

"Uh, went to sleep early. Training."

"That's good. Now listen, Alfred, Mrs. Elversen's gonna need me to stay up here till Thursday.

"Okay."

"You still there, Alfred?"

"Yeah."

"Now you call Dorothy in the morning, before they go to church. Tell her I'll pick up the girls Thursday night. You got that?"

"Thursday night."

"Right. There's no answer there now, they must be at the movies. You sure you're all right, Alfred?"

"Fine and dandy."

"Now don't forget, Alfred."

"Thursday night."

"Right. Bye, now."

"Bye."

He stumbled into the front room and turned on the television set. He passed out before the picture appeared.

He woke once to go to the bathroom, and a cowboy was standing on top of a speeding stagecoach, shooting Indians. He passed out again in the bathroom. When he dragged himself back, the television was humming behind a flickering test pattern. He fell into the couch.

He awoke to organ music. There was a picture of Jesus in long white robes on the screen, and the words "Dawn Devotional" under His feet. Vaguely he remembered that he had to call Dorothy about something, but his body was fastened to the couch. His arms were too heavy to lift. The conga drums were pounding in his head. It seemed like hours before he was able to lift his head, hours more before he could move his arms and legs. Slowly he stood up. The organ music was swelling. He staggered into the kitchen. The clock on the cabinet was ticking off the last few seconds to seven o'clock. With hands as clumsy as boxing gloves, he fumbled a pot out of the stove and filled it with water. He dozed while it boiled away. The smell of the burning pot jerked him awake. He started all over again, spilling the instant coffee powder. It was nearly eight before he had the black coffee in a cup. It was hot and bitter, but it washed away the sandy cotton in his mouth.

The telephone rang.

"You ready, champ?"

"What?"

"Got us a car, Alfred. We're going out to Coney Island, remember?"

"Major?"

"Yeah, man. Be in front of the house in five minutes."

"Don't feel right."

"Ocean air, champ, best thing for you."

"No, I—" Major hung up.

A wave of sickness washed up from his stomach.

"Good morning, Kiddie Klubbers, it's Uncle Harry—"

He rushed in and snapped off the set just as a fat man with a false nose began pouring corn flakes into the screen.

Alfred made more coffee. He gulped it black and

boiling. Mr. Donatelli said never have more than one cup a day, if that much. Smart-meat Donatelli, knows all. I oughta call him up and get a program for hangovers. Outside, a car horn sounded short, sharp blasts. He poured a third cup of coffee. Someone pounded on the door.

"Hollis?"

"We're waitin' on you, Alfred."

"Look, I'm—"

"C'mon, man, you need a break. Been workin' too hard."

Alfred let Hollis lead him downstairs.

On the street, Major waved him into the red-leather front seat of a white Cadillac convertible. Hollis climbed into the back with Sonny and a younger boy Alfred had seen around the neighborhood.

"Who's car is this?"

"Mine," said Major, jerking it away from the curb with a screech of gears. "Loaned it off a guy."

They cruised along the streets, past families dressed for church and winos stumbling out of alleys into the bright morning sunlight. Major lounged behind the wheel, guiding the big car with the fingertips of his right hand. His left arm dangled out, slapping the door in time to music blaring from the car radio.

"Now this is something, ain't it?" He grinned at Alfred.

"Yeah."

Major took his hand off the wheel and plucked a pair

of tinted sunglasses out of his T-shirt pocket. While he was slipping them on, the car veered toward a young couple crossing the street. They scrambled back to the sidewalk.

"Wake up," yelled Major, laughing, grabbing the wheel and straightening the car.

People watched the Cadillac cruise past. Look at them wish themselves into the car, Alfred thought, phony cats with long-playing records under their arms and no machine to play them on. Just hanging around, waiting for something to happen. He leaned back into the red leather.

The car picked up speed, swinging onto a highway. Off to the right, the Hudson River lay blue-green and quiet, glinting under the sun. Small boats churned through the water.

"Now there's some living," said Hollis, leaning forward.

"I'll loan one of them sometime," said Major.

"Hear there's some real parties on those boats," said Hollis.

"You ever know a black man got one of them?" asked Major.

"No."

"They won't let you park it," said Major. "Even if you bought one, you couldn't park it, just have to keep goin' up and down the river. They don't get you one way, they get you another. Right, Alfred?"

"If you say so."

Major laughed. "You all right, Alfred."

The highway narrowed into a tunnel, and Major yelled, "Toll booth." He stretched his left arm toward the back seat.

"Got no change, Major," said the younger boy, "only dollar bills."

"They take dollar bills," said Major. He slowed for the toll booth, took the boy's dollar, and paid. He pocketed the change.

Coney Island was hot and noisy, the streets off the boardwalk choked with boys and girls, white and black, marching up and down, looking each other over. Alfred began to feel cramps in his stomach at the mingled smells of cotton candy, barbecue, fried chicken, and hot dogs. He realized that he hadn't eaten since Friday lunch, nearly two full days ago. He heard distant screams from the thundering roller coaster. Up ahead, a huge Ferris wheel spun slowly against the blue sky.

Major double-parked in front of an outdoor stand. "Go and get some food, Justin. Dogs, French fries, some a that sweet corn. You go help him carry it, Sonny."

"Carry it," said Sonny, climbing out.

"Mustard on the dogs, Major?" asked Justin.

"Everything on the dogs."

Major leaned back in the seat, his arms behind his head. "We'll get us some food, then go find us some pretty little foxes. You got that bottle, Hollis?"

"Cops," said Hollis.

Major and Alfred turned. Two policemen were moving toward them, checking drivers' licenses and registration papers along the row of double-parked cars.

"Don't need that," said Major, starting the car.

"You steal this car?" asked Alfred.

"Gonna return it," said Hollis, "we just . . ."

His words were lost in the sudden roar of the engine. Major jerked the car into traffic. The policemen began to run, shouting, as Major stomped on the accelerator and pounded the horn at people crossing the street. A baby carriage rolled up in front of the car, and Major slammed on the brakes.

"Let's get out a here."

Alfred vaulted over the door, into the gutter, landing hard on his right foot. The ankle twisted under him and he went to his knees, but he got up and plunged into the crowd on the sidewalk, pushing through. Keep moving, keep moving. He ducked his head at the police whistle, and rounded a corner, slamming into a hard chest, and a hand cuffed him on the head. Keep moving, and then he was on the boardwalk, and he slowed down, the ankle beginning to throb, and he let himself be carried along in the flowing crowd. He walked until every step on his right foot sent a shaft of pain up through his ankle. He sat down on a bench.

Thousands of people were jammed together on the beach. He could hardly see the sand. Men and women lay stretched out on blankets. Guys with good builds swaggered among the blankets and umbrellas, slowing down and sucking in their stomachs whenever they

103

passed girls. Babies cried over the noise of transistors. He started walking again, until he found a food stand. He bought spare ribs, buttered corn, French fries, and a Pepsi-Cola. Worst things you can eat, said Donatelli. Alfred gobbled it down as fast as he could. A moment later he was hanging over the boardwalk rail, vomiting.

"Disgusting," said a voice behind him.

"Poor kid."

"A junkie, tryin' to beat it with food, just can't do it, you just can't . . ."

He got away from there as fast as his ankle would let him, stumbling along with the crowd. Shoes kicked at the back of his feet whenever he slowed down. His body itched from streaming sweat. His shirt and pants were damp. He got off the boardwalk, and limped along the strange Brooklyn streets. Every time he passed a policeman he lowered his head and held his breath.

He found a movie house along a wide avenue and went right inside without bothering to find out what was playing. The theater was cool and his stomach quieted down. He bought an ice cream cup and pressed the frosty paper container against his cheeks and temples until the fever in his face disappeared. The ice cream melted, and it went down easily and stayed down. He had another, and began to feel better.

He watched the movie. Handsome, well-dressed white men got in and out of fancy cars with beautiful blond women. For a while, he tried to follow the picture, then gave it up. You all right, Alfred. Thanks, Major, thanks a lot. How long ago now, a month, two months? That last time Major used his fists and feet to bust me up. This time he . . . Don't blame him, man, he didn't pour all that stuff into you at the party. You did that. He didn't put a knife in your throat and make you take a ride. You got in the car. Major was just being friendly. I'll bet, said Henry. If they don't get you one way, they get you another.

He stumbled, blinking, back into the hot street. It was like walking through an invisible curtain. He walked for a long time before he found a subway station. On the platform, people moved away from him, wrinkling their noses. He noticed there was dried vomit on his sneakers.

It was early evening before he got back to Harlem. The nationalist speakers were on their stepladders, screaming into the dying sun. "Tomorrow morning, Monday morning, you wake up, check the baby to see if the rats bit its ears off—"

"You said it, brother."

"—then you go on down to meet The Man . . ."

"Brooksy, hey, Brooksy, wanna talk to you. Heard you been . . ." He crossed the street, not even bothering to pretend that he hadn't heard Harold. I heard you, smart meat, now get lost. This happy little darky just ain't interested.

He walked aimlessly for hours. His ankle throbbed again, but he kept moving. Hungry-eyed faces filled the street corners, waiting for something to happen. Only a few hours left in the weekend, brother. If the action don't come, it'll be another five days before you can get back on your street corner and start waiting again.

He suddenly realized he was on the familiar block of low apartment buildings, a store-front church, a delicatessen, a pawn shop, and on the corner, a bar. The door leading upstairs was slightly open, as usual. A dim light flickered through the dirty plate-glass window on the third floor. He stared at it for a long time. Then he went home.

The telephone was ringing as he came through the door.

"Where you been, Alfred?"

"Major."

"Thought they got you."

"No, I—"

"Listen, man, I don't think there's gonna be no trouble, but if anybody asks where you was today, we all was over your house playin' cards. Got that?"

"Playin' cards."

"Right. You doin' anything now?"

"Yeah." He hung up.

He filled the bathtub with hot water, and stripped off his shoe and sock. The ankle was swollen and soft to the touch. He sat on the edge of the tub and soaked his foot. Couldn't run tomorrow if I wanted to, he thought. As if I wanted to. Knock your brains out, bust your back, run your feet down to the bone. What for? The Man said, nothing's promised you. We know that.

He lay on his aunt's bed with his clothes on, and closed his eyes. It seemed as if it was only a minute later when they opened again. A pink dawn. Running time. His ankle was a little stiff, but the swelling was gone. No pain. He started up, then lay back. Don't need that foolishness. Ain't gonna be a boxer anyway. Run for nothing. The birds are gonna have to get along without old Alfred.

Ben Epstein winked at him when he came into the store. "How was your weekend, Alfred?"

"Real fine."

"One long party, eh?"

"You know."

The day dragged on and on. He sorted the new crates, stacked the canned goods, lugged the filthy garbage pails out back. His muscles felt sore. He went straight home after work and opened a can of pork and beans. He didn't bother to cook it. Cold and greasy, each spoonful dropped to the pit of his stomach and lay there. The phone rang.

"You all right, Alfred?"

"Aunt Dorothy?"

"Just talked to Pearl, she was surprised you didn't call us yesterday. Not like you, Alfred."

"I'm sorry. I forgot."

"All that exercising must really tire you out. Come on out to dinner tomorrow night, been so long since you been here."

"Well, maybe—"

"Jeff's here, you could talk with Jeff and—"

"I'm sorry, Aunt Dorothy, I got something else to do."

"You're going to wear yourself out, all that exercising and running. Take a break and come on out. Jeff won't be home again till Thanksgiving."

"I can't."

"Well, you know you're always welcome."

"Thanks."

He went into the front room and stretched out on the couch. That's all I got to do, go listen to Jeff count up all his opportunities for advancement. Take a break. Hollis said that too. Yeah, I'll take a break. About this time Old Uncle Alfred would be beating at the air in front of a mirror or skipping rope. Like a fool. Good thing nobody ever looked at me much up in that gym or they'd fall over laughing.

He turned on the television and watched it until he couldn't keep his eyes open. Then he slept.

Tuesday dragged along too.

"That must of been some weekend," said Ben, winking.

"Sure."

Late in the afternoon, while he was sweeping the storeroom, he saw Henry limp in through the front door. Alfred quietly slipped out the back door and waited until Henry left. Why can't people just leave you alone, he thought.

He didn't feel like going back to the empty apartment after work. He walked. He passed the clubroom and quickened stride. If I just could have talked James into going to a movie that Friday night. If I just could have thought of something to say at the party when he was looking at me with the junk in his hand. Some partner I am.

He found a triple feature up on 125th Street, and went in. He had seen all the pictures on television already. So what. See them again, see them a thousand times, the new ones are the same as the old ones anyway.

He came out into the night. There weren't too many people on the street. Tomorrow is Wednesday, a working day. Get up, go to work, go home and sleep so you can work some more and pay for your fun on the weekend. And then it's Monday again. Days move so slow. The stores along the avenue were already advertising back-to-school clothes. The summer went so fast. Where'd the summer go? In the park, up in the gym. He walked faster. What makes you think you won't quit this too, Mr. Donatelli said. Smart meat.

He looked up. A dim light flickered through the dirty plate-glass window. How'd I get here? Habit, he thought. He started to walk past the sagging door. Maybe go up for a minute. Might as well clean out the locker.

He took the old steps one at a time, twice stopping to catch his breath. Last time I have to go up these crummy steps. Donatelli was sitting on a folding chair, tipped back, staring out the window. He didn't turn around.

Slowly Alfred stuffed his sweat shirts, trunks, supporters, socks, his secondhand boxing shoes into a paper shopping bag. Maybe I can sell them back to Bud Martin for some new kid who would really use them. He felt tears in his eyes. He looked at the square head, silhouetted against the flickering neon lights. Turn around, turn around. If you don't look now, you never going to see me again. He slammed the locker shut. The clang echoed through the room. The head didn't turn.

At the door, Alfred said, "Good-bye, Mr. Donatelli."

The head barely moved. "Good-bye. Good luck to you."

"Well . . . So long. Thanks."

"You're welcome."

"I'm sorry."

"You've got nothing to apologize to me for."

"Mr. Donatelli?"

"Yes."

"If . . . if I had kept going, would I ever have got any good?"

"Who knows?"

"If . . . if I had wanted to, would I have . . . you know, been a contender?"

"Don't ask me."

"Then who?" said Alfred.

"Yourself. Anyone can be taught how to fight. A contender, that you have to do yourself."

"If I wasn't giving it up, would I ever have got a chance to spar?"

"Probably."

110

"To have a real fight someday?"

"Perhaps."

"Would you know then?"

"Maybe."

"Maybe? Only maybe?" The head didn't move. "When would you know?"

"When you got hurt in the ring for the first time, really hurt. Then I would know."

"Would you . . ." He let the shopping bag drop. "Will you tell me then? When you know?"

"I won't have to, Alfred. You'll know, too."

CHAPTER 13

Left . . . left . . . snap it out . . . drive in . . . mix it up . . . don't let 'im get away, Alfred . . . press . . .

Angel kept slipping Alfred's jab. He cocked his head at the last possible instant and grinned as Alfred's gloved fist shot harmlessly over his shoulder. And each time Alfred missed, Angel belted him in the stomach. There was no pain, only anger that drove his teeth deeper into the mouthpiece. The air exploded out of his nostrils and sweat ran into his eyes. He closed his eyes and swung wildly, and Angel, laughing, belted the side of his head-guard.

"Time," called Henry.

"You're not workin' your combinations," said Bud, pulling out the mouthpiece. "You been throwin' one punch at a time and that's no good."

"But, I—"

"Time," called Henry, and Bud shoved the mouth-piece back in.

Jab-jab-hook . . . jab-hook-right . . . jab . . . hook to

112

the body . . . cross to the chin . . . body . . . head
. . . jab . . . jab . . . jab . . .

August, gasping for breath, melted into September. It
was cooler in the park at dawn now. But it was hot in
the gym, always hot in the gym, the leather headguard
squeezing his temples, the metal protective cup pinch-
ing his thighs. The 16-ounce sparring gloves felt like
lead pillows. Angel slipped the jab, and Denny slipped
the jab, while Henry screamed and Bud yelled, and
sometimes Donatelli watched and sometimes he didn't.

When Alfred remembered his dreams the next morning, they were always the same: A fly was sitting on the
tip of his nose, and every time he reached to brush it
away he saw he had no hands.

"Ten seconds left," called Henry.

Angel's face, framed in the headguard, bobbed up,
mocking him. Last chance for today, thought Alfred.
Now. He snapped out a left jab, straight at the moving
head, just as he had for weeks. And Angel, as he had for
weeks, cocked his head and let it shoot by, never bothering to watch Alfred's shuffling feet. Angel didn't see
the right until it was almost too late. When he jerked his
head away from the right, a left hook slammed into his
face.

Angel's head snapped backwards, his face twisted
with surprise. His gloves automatically flew up to his
face. Alfred dropped his right shoulder, took a quick
step forward on his right foot, and slammed a short
right uppercut into Angel's belly.

113

Alfred plunged forward, the months of shadowboxing taking over now, left . . . left . . . right to the face . . . hook . . . and Angel was reeling against the ropes, a drop of blood oozing from his nose.

"Time," called Bud. Jelly clapped. Pete leaned over the ropes and slapped his shoulder.

"You're thinking," said Donatelli. "Not bad."

Not bad, thought Alfred, spitting the mouthpiece into Henry's hand. That's like a medal from anyone else.

Jose began unlacing Angel's gloves. "Alfred really catch you one, ay?"

"I do it so he feel good," said Angel.

"Nex' time he feel so good he knock you out," said Jose, winking at Alfred. Angel began chattering in machine-gun Spanish.

"You did real good," said Henry, unlacing Alfred's gloves. "That was the best hook you ever threw."

"I'm not sure I know what I did right."

"You been taking a little step before you threw the hook, made you off balance. This time, you pivoted. Like this." Henry threw a slow hook, and pivoted on his left leg. The crippled leg.

"Yeah," said Alfred, practicing it. "Yeah. How'd you know?" He tried to keep his eyes from staring down at Henry's leg.

"I'm learning too, man," said Henry. Then he noticed Alfred's stare, and limped heavily away.

Stick and move . . . in and out . . . jab-jab-right . . . jab-jab-hook . . . jab-hook-right . . . mix 'em up . . . press . . . press . . .

114

Denny's hands were quick, but his footwork was slow. Stand and fight with him, he'll spin your head around. Stick and move, he doesn't have a chance. Sorry, Denny, thought Alfred, my head's not a punching bag for you.

"Time," called Bud.

"You have nice moves, Alfred, very nice moves."

"Mr. Epstein!"

Old Lou smiled. "I have to hear from the neighborhood how good you're getting? So I came up to see."

"Hey, Lightning," said Bud, raising his fists. "You ain't been up for years."

"Don't talk about years. How's my boy doing?"

"Gettin' there, he's gettin' there. You look good, Lou, ready to go ten."

"Ten steps, maybe."

"Sure." Bud clapped him on the shoulders. "Saw Kid Ryan last week, he was askin' for you."

"A rematch I won't give him, even after forty years. A tough one, remember that night . . ."

When Alfred came out of the shower, Bud and Lou were throwing slow, creaky punches in the air, and laughing. He was dressed and half out the door when Lou called, "Wait just a minute, Alfred."

Lou took a little black purse from his pocket, counted out some bills, and pressed them into Bud's hand. "Don't tell Ryan where it comes from, pride he always had."

"Thanks," said Bud. "Take it easy, Lou."

"How else can I take it?" He put a hand on Alfred's

shoulder, bracing himself as they walked slowly down the steps.

On the street, Lou said, "You didn't take my advice."

"Well, Mr. Epstein, I—"

"You should have your own mind, do what you want. Ben tells me it takes you half the time to sort the new stock Monday mornings. How come you suddenly have more energy now?"

"Well, I—"

"Let me figure it out, I have to keep my mind active. You know how to work the register?"

"No. But I could learn."

"Sure you could learn. Maybe come in a little early tomorrow, before we get busy. I'll show you some things."

"Thanks, Mr. Epstein, I'll—"

"Don't thank me, Alfred. I'm not giving you anything you won't have to work for."

Stick and move . . . double-jab . . . double-hook . . . cross with the right . . . hook over the jab . . . slip and stick . . . break clean . . . move 'im, Alfred.

Jose was not as fast as Angel or Denny, but he hit harder. Twice, he fired straight rights through Alfred's guard, stinging, rib-bruising rights that took Alfred's breath away. It wasn't until the third sparring round that Alfred timed the rhythm of Jose's attack, and dropped his left arm, catching the right on his elbow. Jose's face was unprotected and Alfred pumped a fast right into his mouth. He pivoted on his left foot, and threw the hook in a smooth, short arc. Jose dropped like a sack of potatoes. He was back on his feet immediately, but Donatelli jumped into the ring and grabbed Alfred's gloves.

"Better go downstairs," he said softly. "It's time you were fitted for that custom-made mouthpiece."

CHAPTER 14

At 5:30 A.M. his eyelids snapped open. It was gray and chill beyond the kitchen window. For a moment he wished it was just another day, get up, out to the park, suck in the cool October air and listen to his sneakers crackling over the fallen yellow leaves. He tried to close his eyes. He rolled over on his stomach and buried his face in the pillow. A bird somewhere, lonely and lost, called for its friends. He turned over on his back. The green plaster over the kitchen sink had finally cracked loose, leaving a powdery-white hole as big as a fist. He wondered why he hadn't noticed it in four months.

After a while the apartment began to stir—first Aunt Pearl, turning heavily in bed for the last few minutes of sleep, then the girls, drowsily untangling their arms and legs. An automobile horn blared downstairs. Garbage can covers clanged. A policeman, bored and tired, dragged his nightstick along the bars of an iron fence. A skinny shaft of sunlight came through the window.

"You sick, Alfred?"

"Feel fine, Aunt Pearl."

"Ain't you gonna run this morning?"

"Not this morning."

"Oh?"

She washed and dressed and woke up the girls. They began wandering between the front room and the bathroom, their eyes half-shut, bumping into each other. Such nice little girls, he thought, warmth spreading through his stomach. See that they get some real cute dresses one of these days.

"You gonna stay in bed all day?"

"For a while."

"You be late for work."

"I'm off today."

"How come?"

"Just like that."

"You ready for breakfast?"

"Just some tea."

"I suppose you want your tea in bed."

"No, I'll get up for it."

"What's going on, Alfred?"

"Nothing."

She let two pots clatter to the floor. Alfred's head jerked up. "Just wanna be sure you're alive," she said.

He put his hands under his head and watched them eat breakfast, smiling as the girls kept peeking at him over their cereal bowls.

"Is Alfred sick?" asked Charlene.

"Alfred has retired," said Aunt Pearl.

"Is Alfred gonna stay in bed all the time?" asked Sandra.

"Why don't you ask Alfred?"

"Today," he said, slowly, "Alfred Brooks is resting himself for his big opportunity for advancement."

"What he say?" asked Paula.

"He don't know himself," said Aunt Pearl. She dropped a tea bag into a cup and poured hot water over it. She placed the cup on the table.

"You been doing so good at the store. They didn't fire you?"

"They did not."

"You didn't hurt yourself with all them exercises?"

"I did not."

She shrugged. "Guess you just a lazy boy."

"Don't you have any more questions?"

She pressed her lips together to stop a smile. "Us busy people don't have time for quiz shows in the morning."

They cleared the table and put on their coats. Aunt Pearl leaned over the bed. "You got a secret?"

"I do."

"Okay." She smiled down at him. "I hope it's something good. Tell me later?"

"Tonight."

"Fine." She touched his forehead. "Don't let your tea get cold."

He got out of bed very slowly, stretched, and took the tea cup into the front room. He turned on the television set, and sprawled out on the couch. He watched two cartoon programs and part of an old gangster movie. He

was still sipping at the tea, watching an exercise program for women, when Henry knocked on the door.

"You ain't even dressed yet."

"It's only ten o'clock. We don't have to meet Mr.
Donatelli till twelve."

"Yeah, I know. But still."

"C'mon, Henry, I'll make you some tea. Relax you."

He did not begin to feel it himself until they were on
the street. His stomach tightened. His lips moved mechanically to smile back at people he knew. They
stopped in front of Epsteins' and waved at Lou through
the plate-glass window. The old man left the register
and came out.

"You feel good?"

"Fine."

"You look good. Get a good night's sleep?"

"Yeah."

"Okay, I don't want you should stand around on the
street. I'll see you tonight."

"Tonight?"

"Why not?" said Lou, squeezing Alfred's biceps.

Donatelli was waiting for them at the gym. The room,
empty of fighters, seemed huge.

"You have your card?"

"Right here." Alfred opened his wallet and pulled out
the amateur card with a postage-stamp photograph.

"Let Henry hold it."

They followed Donatelli downstairs, stopping at the
second-floor dentist's office.

"I have a patient now, you better eat without me,

Vito," said Dr. Corey. He handed Henry a small box. "I made Alfred a second mouthpiece in case he swallows the first."

"That's not funny, Arthur," said Donatelli.

"So I'm not a comedian." He winked at Alfred. "Don't let these two make you nervous."

Donatelli led them to a small luncheonette around the corner. He ordered sandwiches for himself and Henry, two soft-boiled eggs, toast, and tea with honey for Alfred. The counterman brought the food to their booth.

"You're gettin' to be a stranger, Vito. How's the Streeter kid?"

"I don't handle him anymore."

"Too bad. Got any good ones?"

"They're all good ones."

"Yeah, sure." The counterman laughed.

They picked at their food. "Do you feel butterflies in your stomach?" asked Donatelli.

"No. Like a cold spot."

"That's good. Means you're on edge. The tea will help settle your stomach."

"Henry better have some tea, he's got the butterflies."

The thin lips parted. "That's even better."

On the street again, Donatelli hailed a taxi. He gave Henry a key and three dollar bills. "I'll be up in a few hours. Just make sure Alfred rests." He said something to the driver, and the cab lurched into the uptown traffic.

"Where we going?"

"Spoon's place," said Henry. "Be nice and quiet there."

Alfred relaxed into the back seat. "This is all right. What happens when you turn pro? You get a Cadillac and a chauffeur?"

Henry shook his head. "When Jelly had his first fight, he came back from the weigh-in by subway."

"Hm. Is Jelly gonna fight again soon?"

"I don't know. Just between you and me, Mr. Donatelli ain't so high on him anymore."

"But he knocked the guy out in one round."

"Yeah, but Mr. Donatelli says anybody can't control himself with food can't go all the way. He said that to Jelly's face."

"What Jelly say?"

"He just made a joke, you know Jelly. And then he went out and had a whole chicken. Said he wanted to get an appetite for dinner."

Alfred looked out the cab window. A breeze had sprung up, whipping flecks of white on the Hudson River. The cold spot grew.

"Where's Spoon live?"

"Washington Heights."

"That in Manhattan?"

"Yeah."

Across the river, on a hill, the Ferris wheel of an amusement park stood motionless against a hazy gray sky.

"Henry?"

"Yeah?"

"You know this is the first time I ever rode in a cab."

"When I was a kid, I rode in a lot of cabs."

"How come?"

"My mother used to take me to the clinic in a cab."

"Oh."

"For my leg. I had polio," said Henry.

"Yeah, I know. I been watching you lately, you don't drag your leg so bad anymore."

For the first time Alfred could remember, the grin completely disappeared from Henry's face. He turned away. "Sometimes it gets a little better. Just temporary."

The cab stopped in front of a six-story brick apartment building on a quiet, tree-lined street. Henry paid the driver and limped heavily to the lobby elevator.

There were more books in Spoon's living room than Alfred had ever seen in a home. The walls were covered with book shelves up to the ceiling. Magazines and records were neatly stacked around the room.

"You think he's read all these books?"

"I don't know," mumbled Henry, lowering himself into a soft chair.

"How you feel, man?"

"Me?"

"Yeah. All I got to do is fight tonight. You, the assistant trainer, got to do all the worrying, right?"

Henry brightened a little. "Spoon says he'd never get to read all these books if he lived to be a hundred, but when him and his wife have an argument all they got to do is look it up and see who's right."

"What do they argue about?"

"I was here one time before and she said the first American to get to the North Pole was colored, and he said, No, the colored guy and the white guy stepped on it the same time."

"I never even heard about that in school. Who was right?"

"I don't know. They were still looking it up when I had to go."

Alfred laughed. "Some argument. One time I was over this guy's house and his folks got to arguing about cigarettes, and first thing you know they were throwing bottles."

"Bottles?"

"Yeah. Whiskey bottles. They didn't hit each other, but they hit this guy and he had to get nine stitches in his head."

"Was that James?" said Henry.

"How'd you know?"

"I heard it around. You see him anymore?"

"No. I tried to call him a few times but his folks don't know where he's at," said Alfred.

"You were real tight."

"Yeah. He used to be my best friend."

"What happened?"

"You know how it is. Get older."

"What do you mean, Alfred?"

"Forget it. You ever go down the clubroom?"

"Don't you know what happened? Thought you did. They were having a party down there, couple of weeks ago, making a lot of noise and somebody called the cops. They busted in there and found marijuana and heroin—"

"Was James there?"

"Yeah. Everybody beat it except Sonny, he's so dumb. And some kid named Justin. They got arrested. My father kicked them out. It's just an extra storeroom now."

"Where they all hang out now?"

"They scattered."

Alfred pretended to study the books. Many of them were worn around the edges, as if they had been handled often.

"What you thinking about?" asked Henry.

"Huh? Nothing much. Let's see what's on TV."

Henry got up. "I'll turn it on. You gotta rest." He snapped it on. A woman was giving a lesson in French. "You want to watch this?"

"Why not? I might have to fight a Frenchman someday."

"You don't have to talk to him, just hit him."

"Yeah." Alfred pointed a finger at Henry. "You better watch it. You might have to talk to his trainer or something."

Spoon came in a little after three-thirty, a briefcase under his arm. "I always found the worst part of fighting was those long afternoons, just waiting and killing time."

"You must of read a lot of books then," said Alfred.

Spoon shook his head. "Wish I had. No, I used to play solitaire. There was one fighter in those days, a pretty good light-heavyweight named Junior Ellis, who used to sing along with country and western records before a bout. He said it got his fighting juices worked up."

"What happened to him?"

"He had a fight with a top contender, an Italian kid, and lost. The next day, in the papers, the contender said he won because he sang along with opera."

They were still chuckling when a plump, sweet-faced young woman came in. She was carrying a briefcase too. Spoon got up and kissed her.

"This is my wife, Betty. You remember Henry Johnson, and this is Alfred Brooks."

"I'm glad you came up." She shook their hands. "You men sit still. I just have to put Alfred's steak on, and I'll be right out." She went into the kitchen.

"This is a nice place," said Alfred. "Thanks for letting us use it."

"We like it here. Betty can walk to school, and I drive to mine in about twenty minutes."

"Did you get your permanent license?" asked Alfred.

"You remembered. Yes, I did. I'm taking some courses at night for my master's degree now."

"You teach school and go to school?" asked Alfred.

"The more you learn the more you want to know. You

ought to think about night school for yourself," said Spoon.

"I didn't graduate from high school," said Alfred.

"You can go to high school at night."

"Yeah?"

"Of course. When you're ready, give us a call. Either Betty or I could find out the night school nearest your home. Or you can do it yourself."

Soon, Betty came out in an apron. "It's ready."

The table was set for one. A large steak sizzled on a plate. There was a bowl of salad, two slices of toast, and tea with honey.

"Go ahead, sit down, Alfred. It's for you."

"What about everybody else?"

"We'll eat later," said Spoon, "while you're taking your nap. If you eat a big meal too close to a fight there isn't time for proper digestion. Makes you sluggish and slow, and one good punch to the belly and—"

"Billy!" said his wife.

"She's not the world's greatest fight fan," said Spoon.

The steak was thick and rare. He felt funny eating alone, and offered Henry a piece. But Henry just shook his head, and watched him eat, and once told him to chew more carefully. The Witherspoons chattered about school, and about some boy in Betty's class who suddenly quit doing his homework. When Betty called his mother into school, she found out there was trouble at home. Alfred was surprised that a teacher could care so much about some kid not doing his homework.

128

"You certainly took care of that piece of meat," said Spoon.

"Are you still hungry, Alfred?"

"No, thank you, Mrs. Witherspoon. That was real fine. Thanks a lot."

Spoon stood up. "We'll take a little walk now, give your body a chance to work on that food."

Alfred, Henry, and Spoon strolled around the neighborhood. Men and women were coming home from work in the early twilight. Most of the men were wearing suits and ties.

"A lot of white people live up here," said Alfred.

"This is a fairly well integrated neighborhood," said Spoon.

"You have any white friends?" asked Alfred.

"A few. Some teachers, some college friends, and a boxer with whom I used to train." Spoon laughed. "Once I found out that white boys bled the same color I did I figured I'd let them move into my neighborhood any time."

By the time they returned, Betty had drawn the bedroom drapes and turned down the spread of the double bed.

"Take off your shoes and loosen your belt," Spoon said. "Try to sleep. If you can."

The room was dark, and the murmur of voices outside the door was too low to make out words. The cold spot returned and grew, an ice ball resting in his stomach. He tried not to think about the fight. He took the cab ride again, and thought about Henry, nervous all day and watching over him like a . . . a trainer.

Dishes clattered, and someone said, "Shhh." It sounded like Donatelli. Everybody's been so nice, he thought. I wonder what they'll say if I lose?

The lights snapped on. Henry was beside the bed. "Okay, Alfred, let's go."

Betty shook his hand at the door and wished him luck, and then they were moving quickly, down the elevator, into the darkening street. Donatelli had firm fingers on his arm. They slid into the back of Spoon's car.

"Do you know who I'm going to fight?"

"No. In these one-night amateur shows, the club in charge matches up the fighters at the last minute."

"What if there aren't any other lightweights?"

"That's always a possibility," said Donatelli.

Dr. Corey and Bud were waiting outside the gym. They climbed into the front, Bud carrying his black satchel, an overnight bag, and a large cardboard box.

"What's that?" asked Alfred.

"A third mouthpiece," said Dr. Corey, "in case you swallow the other two."

"Arthur!"

"What's the matter with you, Vito? Laughter is the best medicine."

"Nobody's sick," snapped Donatelli.

Alfred felt the tenseness in Donatelli's arm, pressed against his own, and the ice ball grew larger and colder. There was little traffic on the streets and over the bridge. The ride ended too quickly, in front of a large, shabby building.

"I'll park the car and meet you afterwards," said Spoon. "Good luck, Alfred."

Donatelli showed tickets to a sleepy old man at the door, and led them through a dark corridor into a large, bare room filled with older men, half-naked boys, and cigar smoke. A gray-haired man came over.

"Good to see you, Vito. This your boy?"

"Right. Alfred Brooks."

"Brooks, Alfred." He made a mark on a clipboard. "Strip down to socks and shorts, Alfred."

The boys in the room eyed each other. The older men called to Bud and Dr. Corey, who waved or shouted back, but Donatelli kept his fingers digging into Alfred's arm.

A doctor came over. He thumped Alfred's chest and back, and placed the cool round end of a stethoscope over his heart.

"Your boy's alive, Vito."

"Yeah, yeah," snapped Donatelli, his voice edgy.

The doctor winked and shone a flashlight into Alfred's eyes, ears, and down his throat. "Have you had any recent injuries, illnesses, dizzy spells, diarrhea—"

"Would I bring him here?" said Donatelli.

"Take it easy, Vito," whispered Bud.

"On the scales," said the doctor. "Brooks. Thirty-four and three-quarters."

The gray-haired man marked his clipboard. "Brooks,

131

black trunks."

Alfred turned to Donatelli.

"Don't worry, Alfred, we brought both black and white." He handed a ticket to Dr. Corey. "You're sitting next to Billy."

"You don't want me in the corner?"

"Henry's working the corner tonight."

Dr. Corey grabbed Alfred's hand. "There's an old saying in—"

"Later, Arthur."

Dr. Corey shrugged, and grabbed Henry's hand. "Good luck."

They hurried outside, past a door marked WHITE TRUNKS AND SECONDS ONLY. Bud led them into a room marked BLACK TRUNKS AND SECONDS ONLY. Half a dozen boys sat and stretched out on wooden benches, surrounded by whispering men. More came in as Alfred pulled on the athletic supporter, protective cup, and black trunks Bud handed to him out of the overnight bag. Henry knelt and laced his white boxing shoes.

"Hands," said Bud, opening his black satchel. He took out two long strips of white cloth and a roll of adhesive tape. Bud and Donatelli each wrapped and taped a hand. Alfred studied a printed poster on the wall.

"Close your eyes," said Henry, opening the large cardboard box.

Something soft and nubby slid over his shoulders. "Open."

It was a snow-white terry-cloth robe.

132

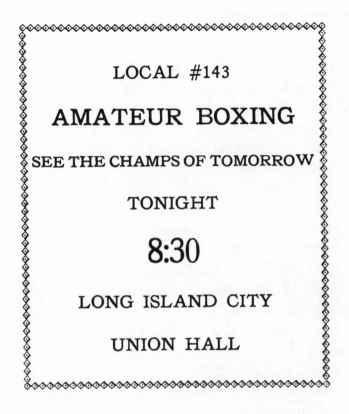

LOCAL #143

AMATEUR BOXING

SEE THE CHAMPS OF TOMORROW

TONIGHT

8:30

LONG ISLAND CITY

UNION HALL

"Show him the back," said Bud.

Smiling, Henry pulled the robe off and turned it around. Written across the back, in red block letters, was ALFRED BROOKS, NEW YORK.

"Hey, man, you look like you just got hit in the face," said Henry.

"Well . . . I . . . I don't . . . I—"

"You got a lot of sweat in your eyes," said Bud, all

gums. He took a sponge from his satchel and patted Alfred's eyes.

"Thanks, I mean . . . I hope—"

"You will," said Donatelli gruffly. "Bud, Henry, let's get the blood circulating, it's chilly in here."

They were massaging his legs and arms when the gray-haired man came in waving his clipboard.

"You go on third, Vito."

"Against who?"

"Kid named Rivera."

"How old is he, what's he weigh, how many—"

"You want to fight or not?"

"Now look, I don't want some—"

"After all these years, Vito, you think I'm going to pull a ringer on you?"

"Easy, man," said Bud. "You know it's nothing personal. We'll take it."

"Sorry," said Donatelli.

"Sure," said the gray-haired man. "I understand." He looked around the room. "Hubbard. Elston Hubbard?"

A powerfully built welterweight with a Marine Corps emblem tattooed in blue on one massive bronze forearm jumped lightly to his feet. "Right here."

"You're on, boy. Jackson, Sam Jackson? You're next." The gray-haired man turned and left.

Hubbard swaggered across the room, two older men trailing him. He turned at the door. "See you cats in a minute," he said, flashing a mouthful of gold teeth.

"That's confidence," said Bud out loud. The fighters and handlers in the room laughed nervously. A tall

134

heavyweight, a little soft around the middle, stood up and began to shadowbox.

"Hands," said Donatelli. He slipped on the gloves, one at a time. Alfred's knees began to quiver.

"How you feel?" whispered Henry.

"Just fine."

The door opened, and the roar of the crowd flooded the room. "Jackson?"

The heavyweight shuffled out with his seconds.

"Stand up," said Donatelli. "Knee bends, that's it, go on down, bounce up, that's the way."

The door opened again, and Hubbard swaggered back in. "Took me one minute, twenty seconds. I'm out of shape."

"Jab," said Donatelli, holding up a hand, palm out. "That's it. Good snap. Let's go."

The ice ball began to melt, trickling freezing water into his legs, stiffening the joints. Donatelli's fingers dug into one arm and Bud's into the other. The crowd noises grew louder as they walked down the corridor and into the back of a square, low-ceilinged meeting hall.

"Ain't Madison Square Garden," said Bud.

"Tonight it is," said Donatelli.

Jackson and another heavyweight were flailing each other in a lumpy, crooked ring in the middle of the hall. Naked bulbs washed the canvas with harsh yellow light. The rest of the hall was in darkness. Alfred couldn't tell how many people sat in the uneven rows of metal folding chairs.

"C'mon, ya bums," someone shouted. The heavy-

135

weights pushed and butted each other clumsily. The referee pulled them apart, and ducked as a long right arm looped over his head. Jackson fell down, and stayed down. He just didn't want to get back up, Alfred thought.

"We're on," said Bud. They started down the aisle, Donatelli and Bud pushing him along with their shoulders. He could hear Henry breathing hard behind them, hurrying to keep up. They waited at the ring steps as Jackson stumbled down, his eyes half-closed, and then they went up, into the pool of hot and blinding light. Bud spread the ropes and Donatelli shoved him through. Rivera was already there, his face blotted out by the lights. He was shorter than Alfred, but very wide and muscular. His legs looked like telephone poles.

"Stick and run, stick and run," whispered Donatelli in his ear, but Alfred was listening to the ring announcer, "In white trunks, from the Bronx, weighing one hundred thirty-six pounds, Joe Rivera. In black trunks, from Harlem, New York, weighing one hundred thirty-four and three-quarters pounds, Alfred Brooks."

The soft, warm terry cloth slipped off his shoulders and Bud's dry stick-fingers were stabbing into his back muscles. "Stick and run, don't slug with him, stick and run, jab and move." Henry shoved the mouthpiece in.

Hands pushed him into the center of the ring and the referee was saying, ". . . three rounds of two minutes each . . . you know the amateur rules . . . break clean . . . shake, boys, and come out fighting."

136

The ice ball exploded, spraying his entire body with freezing, paralyzing streams of water, weighing down his arms, deadening his legs, squeezing his heart.

"Stick and run, don't . . ."

The bell rang. He moved numbly forward on stiff legs. Rivera's beady black eyes stared at him over a bent nose.

"Move, Alfred, for . . ."

He walked right into it, a ton of concrete that slammed into his mouth. His arms flew up, and he staggered backwards on his heels. The ropes burned into his back.

The ice ball was gone.

His legs felt like steel springs and his arms were whips. He bounced off the ropes, flicking the jab ahead of him, pop-pop, into Rivera's face, pop-pop, reddening the bent nose. He moved in with a short right, and Rivera walloped him on the side of the head.

"Stick and run, stick and run," screamed Donatelli.

Alfred danced back, sucking in quick, sharp breaths. Rivera was standing in the middle of the ring, his feet flat on the lumpy canvas, planted like a tree. Alfred circled around him, and Rivera turned, slowly and awkwardly, to keep facing him. Rivera wasn't going to move, he was just going to stand there. I'm going to have to go in and get him, thought Alfred.

"Stick, stick, stick and run," screamed Donatelli, but his voice was lost in a rising chorus of boos.

"Get in there and fight, Brooks," someone yelled, high-pitched and nasty, "Off ya bicycle, go and fight."

137

His body was slick with sweat as he circled Rivera, watching the telephone-pole legs shuffle and turn the squat body. He darted in, pop-pop, and jumped back. Rivera's clumsy left hook missed his head by a foot.

"That's it, Alfred," screamed Donatelli, "just like that, in and out, in and out."

"Fight, ya coward, go in and fight."

"Stick, stick and run."

"Yellow belly, stand and fight."

He darted in again, pop-pop, stand and fight, yellow belly, pop-pop, off your bicycle.

"Move out, Alfred, move . . ."

Pop-pop and he slipped Rivera's slow jab, pop-pop, and he drove in a right cross, stand and fight, and he never saw the punch that slammed into his mouth, snapping back his head. The lights dazzled his eyes, and then a truck crashed into his belly, and a baseball bat blasted the side of his head. He looked up, and the referee was standing over him, wagging a finger, ". . . two . . . three . . ."

The bell rang.

He got up and turned around twice before he saw Bud frantically waving him to their corner. He dropped like a sack on the stool. It seemed like hours before his tongue pushed out the mouthpiece, and then six hands were moving over him, thick, square hands pulling on the elastic waistband of his trunks, "Deep breath, Alfred, deep breath," stick hands stabbing into the muscles of his neck and back, and slim hands tilting the

138

water bottle to his mouth. He gagged on the water and tried to spit it into the bucket in one long stream, but it just gushed out of his mouth over Henry's shoes.

Dimly, he heard the ten-second warning buzzer.

"Stick and run, Alfred," Donatelli whispered into his ear, "don't listen to that crowd, no one's hitting them."

The bell rang.

Rivera was already out there, planted and ready, stick and run, Alfred, stick and run. He darted in, pop-pop, danced back, in and out, in and out, jab and duck, hit and move, circle left, pop-pop, circle right, pop-pop, and he could feel Rivera's blow-torch breaths, hot and heavy against his chest.

"Stand and fight, yellow belly."

Don't listen to the crowd, no one's hitting them, pop-pop, in and out, jab and run away, circle left, and Rivera's eyes were bloodshot and swollen, his thick arms were sagging. Jab and run, dodge, forget the combinations, one punch at a time, two jabs, hit and run, stick and move, don't get too close too long.

"Ahhhhh, go join the track team, Brooks."

The bell rang.

"Smart boxing, Alfred," said Donatelli in his ear, "keep it up, just like that."

"But the—"

"Don't talk, just listen."

The water arched neatly into the bucket. Henry shoved in the mouthpiece. "You won this round, Alfred, it's one each now. Stick and run, stick and run."

The bell rang.

The crowd started whistling, piercing whistles that upset his concentration. Rivera was plodding after him now on slow and heavy feet, pop-pop, stay one step ahead of him, jab and jump away, jab and hook and duck under the swinging arm.

"Run home, ya bum."

In and out, one punch at a time, two jabs, and Rivera was grunting, uh . . . uh, as he tried to find Alfred in the dazzling light and the flying sweat. Pop-pop, hit and run.

"Back to the jungle, ya coward."

The boos flooded the ring and the catcalls burned his ears and the whistles sliced into his brain. Pop-pop, into Rivera's gasping face. A crumpled paper soda cup landed at his foot, and then another.

"Get in there and fight, black boy."

The buzzer sounded, ten seconds to go, pop-pop, get in there and fight, black boy, pop-pop, you slave, and he drove in, pop-pop, hook, Rivera's eyes were wild, pop-pop and right cross.

"Stick and run, Alfred, don't slug . . ."

Jab-jab hook, right . . . left . . . Rivera tried to bring his arms up . . . jab-jab.

The bell rang, and Rivera slammed a short right uppercut into Alfred's groin.

"The winner, by majority decision, Alfred Brooks."

He barely heard it. His legs were soft rubber and a fire was raging in the lower part of his belly. They car-

140

ried him back to the dressing room, and stretched him out on the table. Bud held a small bottle under his nose, and the fumes clawed up into his brain, and cleared his head.

"I'm sorry, Brooks." Rivera was standing over him. "I didn't mean to—"

"Forget it, kid," snapped Donatelli. "Any time a fighter gets hit, anywhere, it's his fault."

The circle of faces grew. Spoon, Lou Epstein, Dr. Corey, Henry, Bud, the gray-haired man, the doctor. Fingers probed.

"Be sore for a day or two, but he's all right."

"You can't listen to the crowd," Donatelli was saying, far, far away, "they just want to see blood and pain."

"Leave the boy alone, Vito."

"But he won, Mr. Donatelli," said Henry. "Alfred won."

"That's not enough."

CHAPTER 15

Aunt Pearl jumped up. "Your face, Alfred, it's all . . . you're limping."

"Looks worse than it is," he said.

"Here, sit down. You want something to eat?"

"Just some milk."

She poured a glass of milk and set it on the table in front of him. She sat down and watched him drink it.

"Want some more?"

"No, thanks."

"You want some aspirin or—"

"I took some already. Doctor gave it to me."

"I'll get your bed ready."

He played with the glass. "Thought you'd have a million questions."

"So you could tell me about the old stone fence off Lenox? A big dog jumped up, right, honey?"

The split in his lip opened again when he smiled. "Yeah."

142

"I had to find out you was having a boxing fight from Mr. Epstein."

"Thought you might try and stop me."

"You gettin' to be a man, Alfred. I stop you from one thing, you'll do something else."

"You said you didn't like my boxing."

"I still don't. Seems an awful shame, two men got nothing against each other go in and try and beat each other's head."

"I don't know about nothing else."

"Before the summer you didn't know about boxing neither."

"I guess I'll have some more milk."

She leaned over his shoulder and filled his glass. "When I was seventeen, Alfred . . . don't look at me like that, I was seventeen, too . . . a man came by the house. He was from the Apollo Theater. Said he heard me singing in the church choir. Wanted to sign me up for a stage show. No star part, you understand, I'd be in a chorus. Wear a fancy dress. They'd teach me some dance steps."

She walked around the table, holding the milk container with two hands. "Was we ever excited, me and Dorothy and Ernestine, your momma. Couldn't sign a contract because I was underage, and my momma, your grandma, wouldn't sign for me. She said that stage shows were sinful. Be shameful, one of her daughters struttin' around, showin' off. I'd end up no good."

She sat down, her fingers tightening on the container.

143

"How I talked with her, and I cried, and Dorothy and Ernestine, they begged her, too. The more we begged the harder she set her face. Sinful. Shameful. No good."

"You never told me 'bout that."

"No secret. You just always been so closed into yourself, Alfred."

"What happened?"

"Nothing. The man went away. I met your Uncle John, and we went together a long time before my momma would give her blessing. She said he didn't have enough money in the bank. How that man worked. Night and day he worked. We got married, and he got sick soon after Charlene came along. He never did get to see the twins. Passed on a month before they came."

Her hands tightened and twisted on the container, and milk spurted out onto her lap. Alfred came around the table and put his hands on Aunt Pearl's shoulders.

"He woulda been real pleased with them. Nice girls," he said softly.

She was sobbing. "I don't say I woulda been a star or anything. I don't know what I'm saying."

"But you would of liked to try," said Alfred.

"Yes."

He held her shoulders until they stopped heaving.

"Thanks, Alfred. You're a comfort." She wiped her eyes and looked up into his. "I didn't even ask if you won your fight."

"I won it."

144

She reached up and stroked his face. "And it didn't even taste sweet, the winning, did it, honey?"

"No."

"You gonna quit this thing now?"

"No."

CHAPTER 16

Griffin was light and fast, his gloves were a red blur tapping away at Alfred's face, easy and steady as rain on a roof, pitter-pat, pitter-pat. Alfred's eyes began to swell and his nose was clogged with dried blood. Donatelli and Henry and Bud were screaming, "Rush him, press, press," but every time he fired out his jab Griffin brushed it aside. By the end of the first round, his face felt as if it had been stung by a hundred bees.

"Attack, attack, two hands," said Donatelli in his ear, and Bud slapped an ice bag against his face. Henry kneaded the muscles of his back. "Go after him, Alfred."

He tried to explain into the ice bag about the red blur and Griffin's speed, but the bell rang. It started again, pitter-pat, pitter-pat, and somebody in the crowd was laughing. He swung wildly, a foot over Griffin's head, and the red blur was back, tapping away at his chin, his eyes, his mouth, his nose. He tried to remember his combinations, left, left, cross, hook, but Griffin's skinny arms knocked his punches away, and then the blur again, pitter-pat, pitter-pat, until he was sure that Griffin had three, maybe five hands at work, all needles and pins stabbing at the bee bites.

The bell rang.

"This is it," said Henry, tilting the water bottle. "Go for the KO, only chance to win, knock his head off."

Pitter-pat, pitter-pat, not quite so fast now, there were only two red gloves, and sometimes he could see them before they tapped against his face. Griffin was breathing hard. He's tired, Alfred thought, tired from hitting me so much. One red glove grazed his ear, the first time Griffin missed all night.

"Rush him, rush him," they screamed from the corner. Somewhere Alfred found a little extra strength, he reached all the way down for it, and the next time the red glove missed he threw his weight behind a short right uppercut.

Griffin stopped cold, a pink blotch on his chest. Alfred swung the hook, everything behind the hook. It slammed into Griffin's jaw. *Thunk*. Pain shot up Alfred's wrist and exploded in his shoulder. Griffin went down and flopped over like a rag doll.

Griffin twitched once, then lay very still on the canvas.

". . . nine . . . ten . . . winner by knockout . . ."

Bud and Donatelli were holding his arms, and Henry was hugging him, but he felt alone and sick. He swallowed back the bitter taste, broke free and ran across the ring.

"Where you goin'?" asked the referee, blocking him.

"Want to see him."

"Later, next bout's coming right in."

"Now," said Alfred, dodging around the referee. Griffin was being pulled to his feet.

"You okay?"

"Huh?"

"I'm sorry I hit you so—"

"Forget it, kid," said one of Griffin's handlers. "Lucky punch."

"Come on, Alfred." Donatelli's fingers were on his arm, pulling him back across the ring. Alfred kept looking over his shoulder as they slapped Griffin awake and helped him down the ring steps.

All the way up the aisle, people stood up and shook their fists and tugged at his robe and cheered. He kept his eyes straight ahead, and his mouth tightly closed. He was afraid he might throw up.

"Let's look at those eyes," said Donatelli, pushing him down on a dressing-room bench.

"Just swollen," said Bud, pressing the ice bag against them. "No damage."

"Beautiful hook," said Henry. "Was that ever a beautiful hook."

"He just lay there—" said Alfred.

"That's part of it," said Donatelli.

"—like a dead man."

"It's happened, Alfred."

Bud took the ice bag away, and looked at Donatelli.

148

They stared at each other for a long time before Bud shook his head, and Donatelli shrugged.

The sound of the hook against Griffin's jaw, the dull, meaty *thunk*, echoed in his mind all the way home in Spoon's car. He heard it in the kitchen, trying to sleep, trying not to see the rag doll flop endlessly to the canvas. He didn't sleep. He left the apartment early, before Aunt Pearl woke up. He didn't want to talk about it over breakfast. He walked through the park, careful to avoid the two policemen. But there was no way to avoid Lou Epstein when he finally went to work.

"Two wins in a row, Alfred."

"Yeah."

"You don't look so good. You want the day off?"

"No, I'm all right."

There were only a few customers that morning. It was hard to concentrate. His fingers were stiff on the cash register keys, and every time he looked up, Griffin was flopping off a shelf of canned goods. *Thunk.* Lucky punch, beautiful hook. Pitter-pat. NO SALE. Pop-pop-pop, and there was Rivera, and the crowd was screaming, get in there and fight, black boy, coward. Twice, he rang up wrong totals and had to call Jake over to unlock the cash register and correct the receipt roll. All the hate was out in the crowd, he thought, screaming for blood, for a knockout, and the crowd didn't really care who flopped over like a rag doll, Griffin, Rivera, Brooks, anybody.

"Go on, Alfred, take the rest of the day off."

"I'm all right, Mr. Epstein."

"Argue I don't, Alfred. You're fired until tomorrow morning, eight-thirty."

He felt a little better on the street. A brisk November wind tugged at his jacket, and he pulled his cap down over his forehead. It was nearly noon, but the sun was neither warm nor bright. The few people on the street were moving quickly. Across the street, in front of a school gate, two heavily dressed figures were handing out leaflets. One of them waved.

"Brooksy, hey Brooksy. Over here."

He shoved his hands into his jacket pockets and strolled over. Harold was smiling, his eyes were friendly behind his horn-rimmed glasses. Lynn seemed very small and slim, bundled into a tweed coat.

"Hi, Alfred," she said. "We were just talking about you."

"How's that?"

She handed him a leaflet. "Harold was saying how much he'd like to get you involved in our new recreation program."

"That's right," said Harold. "The kids would really look up to a boxer."

"Only had two fights."

"That doesn't matter. At least you've done something."

"Don't have much time now."

"Think about it anyway," said Lynn. A bell rang inside the school.

"I will," said Alfred, but Harold and Lynn had already turned and begun handing their leaflets to the children streaming out into the street.

He walked on, surrounded by skipping, laughing children. He thought of Rick, the white college boy he and James had liked so much. Alfred half-closed his eyes, okay you little kids, gonna do some push-ups and trunk-twisters, then James here is gonna tell you some funny stories. But James was trembling in the clubroom corner, ripping open his heroin bag, and the crowd was screaming for him to kill Rivera, and Griffin was flopping over like a rag doll. It was too early to go up to the gym, and he didn't feel like watching afternoon television. He dropped Lynn's leaflet into a trash barrel, and headed toward 125th Street and a warm movie.

CHAPTER 17

Uncle Wilson waved his drumstick. "Two in a row, now that's progress, real progress."

"When's your next fight?" asked Jeff.

"In a week," said Alfred. "And another one a week before Christmas."

"You don't tell me nothing anymore," said Aunt Pearl.

"You worry so much," said Alfred.

"Now, she's got every right to worry," said Aunt Dorothy. "Every day I read in the papers about—"

"Can't hold the boy back," said Wilson. "Top fighter can make contacts with big people, get opportunities."

The room was warm with the nine of them around the table and heat still rising from the turkey, the sweet potatoes, the small mountains of stuffing and green beans. Alfred felt good. Best Thanksgiving ever, he thought, everybody so easy and pleasant, even Wilson. And Jeff was all right, none of those slick, smart-meat college ways he had expected. Lightly he punched Jeff's arm.

"You oughta come up the gym, make a light-heavy out of you."

"I tried it, we had a boxing club in college—"

"You been boxing?" Wilson's drumstick came down in a mound of cranberry sauce. "Get your brains scrambled, waste all that—"

"Wilson." Dorothy pointed at the cranberry stains on his white shirt. The four girls giggled through stuffed mouths, and Pearl raised her napkin to cover a smile.

"I didn't last very long," said Jeff.

"Be glad to show you a few things," said Alfred.

"You forget about that," said Wilson, getting up. He stamped into the kitchen.

"I'd like to be able to handle myself better," said Jeff.

"For Africa?" asked Alfred.

"For anything."

"I hear you talking about Africa?" Wilson came back into the dining room, dabbing at his shirt with a damp towel. "You got accepted and didn't tell me?"

"I haven't sent in the application."

"You better get on with it, boy. Even with your qualifications you can't wait till the last minute."

"I'm not sure I want to go."

"Fine with me," said Dorothy. "I read how they got some tribes running loose over there and—"

"Thought you had your mind set," said Wilson.

"I've been thinking," said Jeff. "All I really wanted to do was see Africa. Now if I really want to do something positive, I can do it right here in this country."

"Didn't bring you up to be no street worker," said

Wilson. "You got the chance to go on out and—"

"Okay. Let's say I go to Africa. Then what?"

"Get a job with a big corporation that—"

"That hires one Negro a year to look good and—"

"Don't you shout at me, Jeff. I know what's best for—"

"Now *you're* shouting, Wilson," said Dorothy.

"That boy just doesn't understand about—"

"Maybe you don't understand," said Jeff.

"Can we go upstairs?" asked Diane.

"Please, please," said the twins.

"Go on," said Dorothy. The girls jumped off their chairs and clattered away. "You men go on inside and behave. No more shouting. Pearl and I gonna clean up the table. We'll call you back for dessert."

Wilson wandered away after his pipe, and Alfred and Jeff went into the front room. They sprawled out on the couch. Jeff wasn't quite so big as Alfred had remembered. Looks a little like Spoon without the broken nose, he thought.

"Are you going to turn professional?" said Jeff.

"Don't know."

"Do you really like to box?"

"Well—"

"I don't mean to be personal."

"You're my cousin. If you can't be personal—" Alfred shrugged.

"I suppose you wouldn't be doing it if you didn't like it."

"I like it all right, especially the running and the

154

workouts. I like the guys at the gym. But sometimes in the ring, I'm not so sure."

Wilson came into the front room, puffing out clouds of pipe smoke. "How you doing at the store, Alfred?"

"Fine. They're real nice to me."

"Might be thinking about the supermarkets, more money, good benefits, chance for advancement."

"I'm not sure I want to work in a store all my life."

"People always gonna need food, Alfred," said Wilson, pointing his pipe stem. "Can't go wrong working in food."

"Sounds like Jelly Belly," said Alfred.

"Jelly Belly?" asked Jeff.

"Friend of mine at the gym. His real name is Horace Marshall Davenport, Junior, but he's so fat everybody just calls him Jelly Belly. Told me once he'd work at Epsteins' for free if he could eat on the job."

Jeff laughed, but Wilson shook his head. "That's the kind of foolishness gets you nowhere, you got to show them you—"

"Come on in," called Dorothy.

There was ice cream and cake and milk and coffee on the table. Wilson sat down and watched his pipe go out. "Always got to be planning for the future, thinking ahead. Wake up one morning and you find the world passed you by." He looked straight at Jeff. "Right, Alfred?"

Alfred leaned back in his chair. "I've been thinking. I'm gonna continue my education."

"Remembered what I said about trade schools?"

"Finish up high school at night," said Alfred.

"You didn't tell me about that," said Aunt Pearl. "When you decide that?"

"Some time now. Spoon says, more you know, more you want to know."

"Spoon?" asked Jeff.

"Alfred's schoolteacher friend," said Aunt Pearl.

They finished their dessert quietly, and watched Wilson clean and refill his pipe. He lit it and puffed out two quick clouds of smoke. He shook his head. "Sometimes I'm not sure I understand this new generation."

"They got to find their own way," said Aunt Pearl. "Same as we did."

"Times are really changing," said Wilson.

"Men like you started the changing," said Dorothy. "Now it's their turn."

"Couldn't do it without you, Dad," said Jeff.

"Maybe so," said Wilson, leaning back. The smoke clouds rose, slowly and evenly.

Aunt Pearl looked at her watch. "We better go. I have to work tomorrow."

"I'll drive you home," said Jeff.

"That's real nice, but—"

"No, I'd like to, Aunt Pearl. It would give me a chance to talk with Alfred some more."

By the time they dragged the girls from upstairs, and thanked each other for the third time, it was past eleven o'clock. Aunt Pearl, Charlene, and the twins piled into

156

the back of Jeff's old Ford, and fell asleep almost as soon as the car started moving.

"Were you serious about finishing high school?"

"Not until I said it tonight. I'm going to try."

"You've changed a lot," said Jeff.

"What way?"

Jeff stared out the windshield at tiny flakes of snow caught, swirling, in the glare of the headlights. "Well, you always seemed so . . . so negative."

"What do you mean?"

"You sort of seemed to, if you don't mind my saying so, seemed to just drift along."

"Yeah. Sweet old Uncle Alfred."

"Sorry, Alfred, I didn't hear what you said."

"I guess I had no ideas about anything, what I wanted to do, anything like that. Didn't seem like any reason to stay in school. And I wasn't doing good. But Spoon says—"

"The teacher?"

"Right. He used to box. He said if you can concentrate on learning to box, you can concentrate on learning anything."

"That makes sense."

"You were talking before about doing things in this country instead of Africa. Like what?"

"For one thing, a lot of groups are trying to organize self-help programs in the black communities. Parents' groups, tenants' groups. . . ."

"Recreation centers for young kids?"

"Very important. White people have always run those centers and they don't always understand the problems. Black children need to look up to black adults."

"They're working on that around our neighborhood."

"You'd be a natural for something like that," said Jeff. "You have all that athletic background."

"You really think so?"

"I'm sure of it."

Aunt Pearl stirred, and leaned forward. "Better turn here, Jeff."

He squinted through the frosting windshield, and guided the car smoothly to the curb. "Here we are."

Aunt Pearl and the girls kissed him, and sleepily climbed out. Jeff shook Alfred's hand.

"I'll be back for Christmas. See you then?"

"Sure. Maybe you'll come up the gym."

"I'd like that."

"Take it easy, Jeff."

The car pulled away, and Alfred pushed the twins toward the stoop. They whimpered in the cold, and began to wake up.

"You two really got on tonight," said Aunt Pearl. "I never saw you talk so much, Alfred."

They started up the stoop. A shuddering old man crouched alongside the stairs, behind a garbage pail. Poor old wino, thought Alfred. He opened the front door. The huddled figure moved, and Alfred suddenly felt sick.

"I'll be right up, Aunt Pearl. I dropped something."

"You'll catch cold, Alfred," she said. The girls started whining, and she herded them inside.

Alfred moved carefully down the snow-slick stoop, and around the side. The lowered head came up.

"I been waiting on you, Alfred."

"I nearly didn't know you, James. You look so bad."

"You gotta help me."

"Come on upstairs with me. I'll get you some—"

"No." The sunken eyes were very bright and feverish. James shivered inside a torn overcoat. "Loan me some money."

"Hot food, James, come on." He grabbed at the overcoat, but James pulled away.

"I need money."

"For a fix? That won't do you no good."

"I'm gonna quit, Alfred, but I need one more, just one more."

"And after that? Come on, James, come on up."

"Money."

Alfred fumbled in his wallet. He had six dollar bills. A clawlike hand snatched them.

"James, wait, please. I'll—"

But James was weaving down the street, almost running. Alfred watched him until he disappeared around the corner. I should of dragged him up, he thought. What's gonna happen to him now?

CHAPTER 18

Barnes wasn't as strong as Rivera or as quick as Griffin, but he was rough and dirty in the clinches. He held Alfred's arms, stepped on his toes, pounded his kidneys. Donatelli screamed, "Break loose, push away," but Alfred's arms were heavy, his legs glued to the canvas.

"What's wrong with you?" snarled Donatelli. Water gurgled into his mouth as Alfred tried to think of an answer. Six hands moved over his body, the ice bag slapped against the back of his neck.

The crowd was booing, but he didn't care. If you want to see blood, he thought, go punch each other. He felt tired, his brain felt tired, his eyes were watering. He threw out his jab mechanically, just stiff enough to keep Barnes away. Once, Barnes tried to duck the jab, and stumbled, his unprotected face bobbing up six inches from Alfred's right fist. "Nail 'im," screamed Henry, but Griffin's twitching body flashed in Alfred's mind, and he never threw the punch.

Barnes clinched and started pounding on his kidneys

again. Alfred looked over Barnes' shoulder at the clock on the far wall. Another thirty seconds. The referee pulled them apart, and Alfred kept Barnes away with the jab until the final bell rang.

". . . decision of the judges . . . a draw. . . ."

The crowd booed him back to the dressing room. Donatelli and Bud and Henry and Spoon and Dr. Corey shifted from foot to foot as he dressed. He avoided their eyes. The ride back to Manhattan was silent. Spoon stopped at the gym first, to let Donatelli out.

"I want you to come up, Alfred," said Donatelli.

They walked slowly up the sagging stairs. Donatelli unlocked the gym door, and went into the darkness to find the light string. When Alfred went in, Donatelli was standing under the single naked bulb, his face smooth and hard. Like the first night, Alfred thought. Donatelli put his arm across Alfred's shoulders. His voice was soft, almost gentle.

"It's time, Alfred."

"You want me to quit?"

"To retire," said Donatelli.

"What about the next fight?"

"I'll cancel it."

"Why?"

"You don't have the killer instinct, Alfred, the coldness to beat a man into the ground when you sense his weakness. I'm not sure I'd want you to have it."

"Not all boxers have it."

"Some are so good they don't need it. You're not that good."

"I could try."

"You did, Alfred." Donatelli raised one bushy white eyebrow. "You don't really like to fight, do you?"

Alfred lowered his head.

Donatelli took his arm away and walked over to the plate-glass window. "I'll never forget how you came up those dark steps. Alone. At night. Scared. You conquered your fear. You worked hard. You almost quit once, and then you came back and worked harder."

"Mr. Donatelli?"

"Yes?"

"Remember what you said that night . . . about being a . . . a contender?"

"Yes."

"You weren't just talking about boxing."

"You understood that."

"And what you said about quitting before you really tried."

"You've tried. I know you've tried."

"The next fight, I—"

"No. You've had three fights now and never lost. They won't match you with the Riveras and the Griffins and the Barneses anymore. They'll put you in with someone who could hurt you, really hurt you."

"Be like not finishing."

"That's not true. You've learned to work hard, to concentrate. To climb." He left the window and came back to Alfred's side. "I'd like you to keep training, keep running, spar with the new boys coming up. Like Spoon does. But no more fights."

"You got to let me finish."

"There are other things you want to do now, aren't there, Alfred?"

"Yes."

"You'll do them. I know you will," said Donatelli.

"Got to finish."

"But why?"

"So I can know, too."

CHAPTER 19

"**Y**ou are nervous," said Henry.

"Always nervous before a fight. Means I'm on edge. Ready."

"Sure. And you always read books upside down."

Alfred pushed the book into the shelf, and dropped back into one of Spoon's overstuffed living-room chairs. "What time is it?"

"Five minutes after it was last time you asked."

"What was that?"

"It's two-thirty," said Henry.

"Exactly two-thirty?"

"Two minutes before two-thirty, all right?"

"Why don't you say so?"

Henry shrugged himself deeper into the couch.

"Man, you are something. Want some tea?"

"No."

"Play cards?"

"No."

"Want to see some TV?"

"I don't care."

"Maybe we'll get another French lesson," said Henry.

"Yeah. Maybe you'll train a Frenchman someday."

Henry brushed some invisible lint off his knee. "I'm sorry, Alfred."

"What are you sorry about?"

"Gonna be your last fight."

"Yeah."

"Maybe if you—"

"No chance. Mr. Donatelli said even if I win big, it's all over," said Alfred.

"You gonna keep coming up the gym?" asked Henry.

"I guess so."

"Alfred?"

"Yeah?"

"Why you so nervous?"

"Told you. Always nervous before a fight."

"But it don't matter."

"Matters to me."

"Alfred?"

"Yeah."

"Tell you something?"

"What's that?"

"Remember that time you said I wasn't limping so bad anymore?"

"*Do* I? You looked like I kicked you in the belly."

"You were right. I don't limp so bad anymore."

"Why's that?"

Henry began brushing both knees at once. "Don't

think about my leg so much. Since I started working for Mr. Donatelli and helping train you, it just don't bother me so much. Sound weird to you?"

"Don't sound weird at all. You gonna keep training boxers?"

"Yeah. Mr. Donatelli says he wants me to start working with new kids coming up soon as—" Henry closed his mouth.

"Soon as you don't have to spend so much time with me. Right?"

Henry nodded.

"That's okay." Alfred stretched out his legs, and worked his hands into his pockets. "Only got to use my robe three times. Keep it clean tonight and you can take my name off, use it for somebody else."

"That's your robe."

"I won't need—"

"Your robe. I bought it for you."

Alfred sat up. "You bought it?"

"Yeah."

"I always thought it was Mr. Donatelli. You bought it?"

Henry smiled, a nice easy smile, nothing like the old plastered-on grin. "You were my first fighter. You got me my start."

"You had the job."

"Just to clean up around the gym. You were the first fighter I helped train. The first time I got to work a corner was for you. I'll never forget you, Alfred."

They sank back into their seats, and stared at specks of dust climbing and circling in a weak shaft of winter sunlight. Henry was quiet, barely moving. Alfred concentrated on the little cold spot growing in his stomach. He wondered if he would ever feel it again, for anything.

"Are you guys hypnotized?" Spoon burst into the apartment, peeling off his overcoat and throwing down his briefcase in one movement. "Did I have a day and a half today. Boy pulled a knife on me in the school yard."

"You knock him out?" asked Henry.

"No. Poor kid had enough beatings in his life. I spent the afternoon trying to explain to him why that knife isn't going to do him any good. It was like going ten rounds." Spoon loosened his tie. "He told me he's scared to walk around without a knife, so I suggested he go down to the gym and look up either of you two guys. His name is Herbert Davis."

"I'll watch for him," said Henry.

"Good." Spoon opened his briefcase, and pulled out some sheets of mimeographed paper. "I got that night-school reading list for you, Alfred."

"Thanks." Alfred stood up, and took it. "Lot of books."

"You can get a start before the semester begins," said Spoon. "We have most of the books here. If you come up next week, when Betty and I are off for Christmas, we can go over them together."

Betty bustled in a few minutes later, and started chattering with Spoon about her day at school. Alfred folded the list carefully and slipped it into a pocket. He closed his eyes and tuned out the chatter. He concentrated on the cold spot again. Got to remember the feeling, he thought, it's like an old friend you're never going to meet again. New friends coming up, new things to do, but never that cold spot growing in your stomach, telling you you're on edge, ready for something big, streams of chilly water running all over your body, and exploding when you have to get in there and fight.

"Steak's ready."

He ate slowly, tasting each bite, a little sorry to swallow because then there was one bite less of the last steak. They took their walk slowly too. Henry and Spoon said nothing, letting Alfred think his thoughts. The last walk.

Spoon led him into the darkened bedroom, and closed the door behind them. "I talked to that doctor at the narcotics clinic, Alfred. He can find a place for your friend. But he says that you'd have to do most of the work. Even after an addict takes a cure, he needs a great deal of encouragement to stay off drugs."

Alfred pulled off his shoes, and lay down. "I can't find him. He cut out of the neighborhood again."

"Let me know when he turns up." Spoon left.

Alfred stared up at the ceiling, at the white streaks that flashed overhead when cars passed on the street below. The cold spot became an ice ball, just like the first time he had lain on this bed, staring at this ceiling, listening to the murmur of voices outside, the soft clink of glasses and dishes. Long time ago, that first fight. A million years.

The light snapped on. Henry looked sad. "Let's go, Alfred."

At the door, Donatelli's pale blue eyes searched Alfred's face, but the thin lips never moved. They filed slowly out of the apartment. Alfred turned at the door and took Betty's outstretched hand.

"Thanks for all the steaks. They were real fine. Goodbye."

She patted his hand. "When you come next week I'll cook something different. And we'll eat together for a change. Good luck."

They all found things to stare at in the elevator, and they each looked out a different window as Spoon drove downtown. Even Dr. Corey had nothing to say when he and Bud climbed into the car in front of the gym.

He tried to remember every little thing so he could store it away for later, the ticket man nodding them into the building as if it was just another fight night, the other boxers looking him up and down in the dressing room as if he'd be an opponent some day, the extra care Henry and Bud took winding the cloth strips around his hands.

"How's your stomach?" asked Donatelli.

"Cold."

"Good. I'd be worried if it wasn't."

The door opened. "Brooks? You go on in the second bout."

"Against who?" asked Donatelli.

"Kid named Hubbard, only one in your class."

"Elston Hubbard?"

The man looked at his clipboard. "That's the kid."

"Forget it." Donatelli stood up. "You can untape Alfred's hands, Henry."

The man stepped into the room. "You don't want the fight?"

"Not against Hubbard."

"Wait now." Alfred pulled his hands away from Henry. "I want the fight."

"No, you don't," said Donatelli. "Hubbard's twenty-two, twenty-three, at least seven pounds—"

"I want the fight."

"You'll get hurt," said Donatelli.

The man tapped his clipboard. "Well?"

"Just one minute, mister," said Alfred. "Look, Mr. Donatelli, remember how you said the only way you'd ever know is if I got hurt, really hurt in the ring?"

"But it doesn't matter now."

"Does to me."

"You don't have to prove anything to me, Alfred."

"To me I do."

A red flush crept up Donatelli's close-shaven cheeks. "You'll have to get yourself another manager, Alfred, one that doesn't mind a little blood."

170

"You're my manager, and you're gonna be in my corner."

"What makes you so sure?"

"You're not gonna walk out on me now. You took me this far, you told me all that stuff about being a contender, and you ain't quitting on me now, not when I got a chance to find out, my last chance—"

"It's not your last chance."

"In boxing it is."

The man rapped his clipboard against the door. "You can argue all night, but I got a program to—"

"All right," snarled Donatelli. "Put us on second."

"Hands," said Bud.

They slipped on the gloves and laced them tight.

"Jab," said Donatelli, holding up his palm.

The ice ball was gone, completely gone, and Alfred had trouble finding his voice. It finally came out high and thin. "You understand, Mr. Donatelli, I got to."

"I understand. Jab."

He swung his arms, and loosened up his legs. The door opened again. The crowd was booing outside.

"Brooks?"

"We're ready," said Donatelli.

They went down the aisle three abreast, Donatelli and Henry moving him along with their shoulders, Bud right behind with the towels and the bucket, up the ring steps and through the ropes. Elston Hubbard was already in the ring, flexing his forearm muscles so the Marine Corps emblem jumped on the smooth bronze skin. The ring lights glinted off his gold teeth when he grinned at Alfred and then out at the crowd. Hubbard held up his right arm, and the crowd cheered.

Just before the bell, Alfred thought he heard Donatelli whisper, "Be careful, Alfred," but it was lost in the roar of the crowd and Henry's scream, "Look out."

Hubbard's face was on top of him and something slammed against the side of his head. The canvas floor came up and smashed into his nose.

". . . three . . . four . . . five . . ."

A gray shirt and a black bow tie hovered above him, and a forefinger waved in his face. ". . . six . . . seven . . ."

He got up.

The referee grabbed his gloves and wiped them off on his gray shirt. "You okay, boy?"

"Yeah."

"What's your name?"

"Alfred Brooks."

"Okay, go on and fight."

Hubbard rushed out of the corner, swinging his left like a meat hook. Alfred sidestepped and snapped a left jab into the charging forehead, then another, pop-pop, but the head came on and crashed into his mouth, hurling him against the ropes. Concrete gloves hammered into his stomach, his sides. The ropes burned across his back. Hubbard's hard body forced him backwards, Hubbard's shoe tips slashed at his ankles, knotty shoulders bumped up into his chin, and the bullet head

172

ground into his eyes. Hubbard was pummeling his ribs now, and Alfred worked his left arm free and began banging at the side of the bullet head, again and again and again, until Hubbard straightened up. Alfred lunged forward on his left foot, and spun away from the ropes. He leaped into the center of the ring.

Far, far away, someone was yelling, "Stick, stick, stick and run . . ."

Up on the balls of your feet, chin in, here he comes, left, left, pop-pop, circle, left, shift, cross. An iron pipe rammed into the pit of his stomach, turning his legs to rubber. *Whomp.* He never saw the punch, but he heard it thud against his ear and then the distant plop, like a stone splashing into the pool at the bottom of a sewer hole. He staggered, dizzy, a sudden coolness deep in his ear.

". . . four . . . five . . . six . . ."

He got up.

"Where are you, boy?"

"Parkway Gardens. Brooklyn."

"Okay."

Left . . . left . . . hook . . . cross, once he thought Hubbard's head jerked back, but then the iron pipes were ramming into his stomach, one after another. Drop your elbows. *Whomp.* He went backwards on his heels, into the ropes. Here he comes, left . . .

The bell rang.

His tongue filled his mouth. Henry had to pull out the mouthpiece, and the cold sponge turned hot on his face.

173

Whatever Donatelli was whispering into his ear fell right to the bottom of the sewer hole, plop. Black stick fingers smeared yellow paste on his eyebrows, stinging him awake.

The bell rang.

Up on the balls of your feet, chin in, stick and run, stick it out, jab and move. Why don't they turn out those lights, blinding me, here he comes, stick, stick, uh . . . Hubbard drove him into the corner, the wooden post slammed into the back of his neck. Hubbard was marching in place, like a soldier, marine, pounding, pounding, iron pipes, sledgehammers, belly, chest, throat, chin. Keep doing it, man, keep doing it. If you stop now I'll just go down, melt down like butter and leak right off the canvas. *Thunk.*

". . . six . . . seven . . . eight . . ."

He got up.

"Had enough, boy?"

"Fine, I'm fine."

"Who you fighting?"

"Elston Hubbard."

"What round is this?"

"Round two."

"Okay."

Stick, stick, cross, hook, pop-pop, he never stops, pop-pop. They clinched in the center of the ring. Hubbard raked his laces across Alfred's rope burns, and stepped on his toes, and rubbed his jaw against Alfred's, the stubble of his beard like sandpaper on Alfred's skin. He threw Alfred away, across the ring, and rushed after him, swinging. Iron pipes again, sledgehammers, meat hooks.

The bell rang.

"You want him to continue?" asked the referee.

Donatelli's pale blue eyes were narrow.

Henry's voice, shrill and loud. "Gotta let him, Mr. Donatelli, gotta."

"Let him fight," said Donatelli.

The bell rang.

The crowd was roaring deep in its gut, ocean waves that lapped at the ring, that drowned all pain and all feeling, drowned all sound but the drumming of leather against flesh. Everything was wet and sticky. Everything was sweat and blood. There were three Hubbards now, all of them hazy, jab at the middle one, hook the middle one. They stood toe to toe in the center of the ring, whacking, slugging, thumping back and forth, flinging sweat, elbows, fists, knees, jab the middle one, hook the middle one. *Thunk.* Alfred felt his mouthpiece fly out, hook the middle one, pop-pop, iron pipes, sledgehammers, meat hooks, go ahead, throw everything you got, you gonna have to, gonna stand here all day and all night and take what you got and give it right back, gonna hang in forever, gonna climb, man, gonna keep climbing, you can't knock me out, nobody ever gonna knock me out, you wanna stop me you better kill me.

The bell rang, but neither of them heard it, grunting,

175

straining, slugging, and then everyone was in the ring pulling them apart, grabbing their gloves.

". . . by unanimous decision . . . Elston Hubbard."

The referee held up Hubbard's right arm, and his manager held up the left, but Hubbard broke loose and ran across the ring, throwing his arms around Alfred. They hugged each other, crying because it was over, and Hubbard gasped, "You tough, baby."

All the way up the aisle, people were reaching out to touch Alfred's robe. "Great fight, kid . . . beautiful . . . real heart, Brooks . . ." The dressing room was jammed, Lou Epstein clutching his gloves, "Like the old days, like the . . ." Jose and Angel screaming, Spoon reaching for him, Jelly and Pete Krakover, Denny slapping his back.

"Let him breathe," bellowed Bud, pushing them all out and slamming the door shut. Henry began to unlace his gloves.

Three Donatellis peered down into his face, then two. His eyes finally focused. The thin lips were parted. Donatelli was smiling.

"Now you know, Alfred. Now you know, too."

CHAPTER 20

Aunt Pearl's hands were clenched and her eyes were wide when he bounded into the apartment.

"Shoulda called and told you I'd be so late." He smiled through cracked lips. "We all went out, Mr. Donatelli, Spoon, everybody. Jelly's got this new job at a fancy restaurant, number-three vegetable man, six round meals a day, he says—who wants square meals—and we all—"

"Alfred, the—"

"Don't mind all this tape on my face." He kissed her damp forehead, and peeled off his coat. "Looks worse than it is, I feel—"

"—police were here."

"Police?" He let his coat and cap fall to the kitchen floor. "What for?"

"They're after James."

"What's he done?"

"He broke into Epsteins' tonight, right through the front window. They saw him, but he got away."

"Why they come here?"

"They were very nice and all. They knew from last time you and James was friends."

"Right through the front window?"

"Why'd he do a fool thing like that, Alfred?"

He shrugged. "Well, I hope he gets away."

"I don't think he's gonna."

"Why not?"

"The police said he cut himself real bad getting out again. Blood all over. They said he can't get too far."

"James," whispered Alfred.

"Police said they think he's a . . . Alfred, where you . . . ALFRED!"

He took the steps two, three at a time, stumbling twice, and he hit the icy stoop off-balance, tumbling into the street, but he was up and running hard, into the bitter night wind that lashed at his thin sweater and blew wet flakes of snow into his face, running out the stitch that chewed at his side, running into his second wind, feeling the cold spot grow and explode in his stomach. He didn't slow down until he reached the park.

The park lay white and silent, the new-fallen snow glistening under a full moon. The snow deadened his careful footsteps, over the smaller rocks, over the low thicket of leafless bushes. He dropped to his knees in the shadow of the huge rock, and elbowed his way through the stunted trees. At the mouth of the cave he heard heavy breathing.

"James," he whispered.

The breathing stopped.

"It's me. Alfred."

"What you want?"

"Come to help you," said Alfred.

"Just go 'way."

He moved in closer, his knees quivering as the snow seeped through his trousers.

"Go 'way."

"My cave, too, James. Remember?"

He crawled in. A wooden match flared, and he saw James, crouched like a cat, his eyes wide, sweat bubbling on his face. Before the match burned down into James' fingertips, Alfred saw the dark, widening stain on his torn coat sleeve, and the blood running off his hand.

"You're cut bad."

"That's my business."

"Need to go to a hospital. I'll take you."

"Leave me 'lone."

"If you don't bleed to death, you could get infected."

"Too bad."

"This ain't the movies, James. You could lose your arm."

The breathing began to slow down, grow shallower.

"James?"

"It hurts."

"Let me wrap it up."

James lit another match. Alfred ripped off the torn coat sleeve and tied his handkerchief around the cut. The handkerchief turned red, but the flow of blood slowed down.

"All that tape on your face."

"Had a fight tonight," said Alfred.

"You win?"

"Sort of."

"You a fighter. Always so meek and quiet."

"Let's go."

"You got any money, Alfred?"

"For a fix?"

"You said you was gonna help me."

"That's not gonna help, just mess you up more."

"Just one more."

"You said that last time."

"What do you know?" James began to sob, his shoulders heaving. Dirt and pebbles spilled off the ceiling of the cave.

"You can beat the junk, man, I'm gonna help you beat it," said Alfred.

"I ain't hooked. I can stop any time. Just one more."

"Look at you, like a garbage rat. You hooked all right. But you and me can beat it."

"It's no use."

"Remember Mosely of the Jungle and Bad Brooks?"

"No."

"Sure you do. Remember how we used to hide here? Remember the night my momma died and you stayed with me, told me you were gonna stick with me? Sure needed you that night."

"I got chills."

"You and me, James. Gonna stick with you. I got

friends, Henry and Bud and Mr. Donatelli, help get you in shape after you beat the junk. Spoon, you'd like him, got more books than anybody."

"It ain't no use." The voice was soft and weak.

"I'm gonna go to night school. You come too. Gonna work in a recreation center for little kids, you come help me. You was always so comical. Get you a job."

"Grocery boy," said James.

"For start. Nothing's promised you, man, but you ain't gonna know nothing till you try. Maybe get to build things like you always wanted."

"Whitey ain't gonna—"

"Dare him to stop you. Dare anybody if you and me partners again."

"I'm too sick. I need a fix."

"Gonna take you to the hospital now."

"They'll call the police."

"Can't do nothing about that."

"I'm on probation, they'll send me away this time."

"Maybe, maybe not. Mr. Epstein'll help if I ask him. Even if they send you away, won't be forever. I'll be around. Gonna get you clean, man, and gonna keep you clean."

"Alfred?"

"I'm right here."

"Why you wanna do all this?"

"Because I know I can, James. And you're my partner. Ready?"

There was no answer. Alfred's fingers moved up

James' arm. The blood was flowing again. "That's the way you want it, James. I'm gonna go. Good luck."

He began edging backwards out of the cave, scraping his feet as noisily as he could. "So long, James."

"Alfred?"

"Yeah?"

"Okay."

Alfred scrabbled back in, reaching, feeling James' outstretched arms around his neck. Slowly, he pulled James out of the cave into the biting wind.

"Easy, man, you be all right." He lifted James to his feet and half-carried him through the stunted trees. James moaned.

"Hang in there, James. Can you walk?"

"Try." He leaned heavily on Alfred. "Weak as a baby. Lost all that blood."

"Don't worry about that, James, I got plenty of blood for you." Carefully, Alfred guided him over the rocks and the bushes and the new snow, toward the lights of the avenue.